The Best Werewolf Short Stories 1800-1849

Φ

A Classic Werewolf Anthology

Edited and Introduced
by
Andrew Barger

University of
Hertfordshire

College Lane, Hatfield, Herts. AL10 9AB
Information Hertfordshire
Services and Solutions for the University

For my youngest daughter, Sage.

"The Ancient English Romance of William and the
Werwolf," Frederick Madden, Title Pg., 1832.

EDITED AND INTRODUCED
BY
ANDREW BARGER

The Best Horror Short Stories 1800-1849
A Classic Horror Anthology

Edgar Allan Poe
Annotated and Illustrated Entire Stories and Poems

Leo Tolstoy's 20 Greatest Short Stories
Annotated

Orion
An Epic English Poem

FICTION

Coffee with Poe

Φ

ANDREWBARGER.COM

BLOG: SCARY-SHORT-STORIES.BLOGSPOT.COM

The Best Werewolf Short Stories 1800-1849
Φ
A Classic Werewolf Anthology

Edited and Introduced by
Andrew Barger

First Edition
Manufactured: United States or United Kingdom
ISBN: 978-1-933747-25-5

Printed on 100% recycled paper in both
the United States and United Kingdom
(20% Post Consumer Waste)

Fonts: Bookman Old Style, CloisterBlack, Times New Roman

CONTENTS

Shapeshifting the Werewolf in Literature

My hunt for the best werewolf short stories published between 1800-1849 in the English language was difficult. This is largely because the werewolf short story was in its infancy during this period. All great monsters of our modern literature germinated, at some point, out of superstitions; from superstitions they grew into the saplings of folklore, and from folklore into the redwoods of legend and finally into great literature. Werewolves are no different.

At the beginning of the 19th century legend of this monster existed in the Greek, English, Italian, German and French tongues. In each, varying names were used for what we today call a "werewolf." The devil or sorcerers were typically the cause of werewolfism. In Vol. I, page 98 of *The Menageries: Quadrupeds*, published in 1829, we find the following passage in reference to Verstegan's *Restitution of decayed Intelligence in Antiquities concerning the most noble and renowned English Nation*, Antwerp, 1605.

'*Were-wulf:* this name remaineth still known in the Teutonic, and is as much to say as man-wolf— the Greek expressing the very like in Lycanthropos. The *were-wolves* are certain sorcerers, who, having anointed their bodies with an ointment which they make by the instinct of the devil, and putting on a certain inchanted girdel, do not only unto the view of others seem as wolves, but to their own thinking have both the shape and nature of wolves, so long as they weare the said girdel; and they do dispose themselves as very wolves

in wurrying and killing, and waste of humane
creatures.'

In reference to German legends of the werewolf,
The Menageries: Quadrupeds, continues:

> The Germans had a similar superstition;
> and, as late as 1589, a man was executed in
> the Netherlands under the charge of being a
> were-wulf. This pretended sorcerer, assuming
> one of the most formidable shapes of mischief,
> was called, in France, *loup-garou*. It is said
> that the wolf, when it has once tasted human
> flesh, gives it the preference over all other
> animal food; and from this cause it probably
> arose that, for many centuries of ignorance,
> when the influence of evil spirits was
> universally believed, and the powers of
> witchcraft were not doubted even by the
> learned, a raging wolf, devouring every thing
> in his way—the sheep in its fold, and the child
> in its cottage bed,— and even digging up
> newly buried bodies from their graves, should
> be supposed to be possessed with some
> demon more fearful than its own insatiate
> appetites.

Great Britain took the legends and superstitions of
werewolves a step further. On page 397 of *The Living
Age* Vol. V of 1845, there is the following passage:

> The common peasant, who alone knows
> anything about the animal, is withheld by
> superstition from even mentioning the name
> of *wolf;* and if he mentions him at all,
> designates him only as the "old one," or the
> "grey one," or the "great dog;" feeling, as was
> also the case in parts of Great Britain with
> regard to the fairies, that to call these animals
> by their true name is a sure way to exasperate

them. This caution may be chiefly attributed, however, to the popular and very ancient belief in the "*Wär Wolf;*" not a straightforward, open-mouthed, plain-spoken beast, against which the cattle may plunge, and fight, and defend themselves as best they may, and which either wounds or kills its prey in a fair and ferocious way; but that odious combination of human weakness and decrepitude, with demoniacal power and will, which all nations who have believed in have most unjustly persecuted and most naturally hated—in other words, a bad, miserable old woman leagued body and soul with Satan, who, under the form of a *Wär Wolf,* paralyses the cattle with her eye, and from whom the slightest wound is death. Be this as it may, the superior intelligence of the upper classes is to this day occasionally puzzled to account for the fate of a fine young ox, who will be found in the morning breathing hard, his hide bathed in foam, and with every sign of fright and exhaustion, while, perhaps, only one trifling wound will be discovered on the whole body, which swells and inflames as if poison had been infused, the animal generally dying before night. Nor does the mystery end here; for, on examining the body, the intestines will be found to be torn as with the claws of a wolf, and the whole animal in a state of inflammation, which sufficiently accounts for death.

Werewolves leaped from legend into the literature through poetry. The famous Roman poet, Publius Ovidius Naso (more commonly known as "Ovid"), gave mention to the werewolf two thousand years ago in Book I of his "Metamorphoses" that signifies a transformation in its very title. In the poem a Lycaon man is so ferocious as a wolf he is deprived of ever attaining the human form again by Jupiter. Consider this translated Latin text from "The first book of Ovid's Metamorphoses, with a literal interlinear translation" of 1828 starting at the end of line 230:

Ille,
He,

territus fugit, nactus-que   silentia   ruris,
terrified flies, and-having-gained the-silence of-the-country,

exululat, conātur-que   frustrà loqui: os
howls-out, and-endeavours in-vain to-speak: *his*-countenance

colligit rabiem ab   ipso,   vertitur-que   in
collects rage   from himself, and-he-is-turned against

pecudes cupidine solitæ   cædis;   et nunc quoque
the-cattle by-desire of-wonted slaughter; and now also

gaudet   sanguine. Vestes   abeunt   in   villos,
he-rejoices in-blood. *His*-garments pass-away into hairs,

lacerti   in   crura. Fit   lupus, et servat   vestigial
his-arms into legs. He-becomes a-wolf, and preserves the-traces

veteris   formæ. Est   eadem   canities, eadem
of-*his*-ancient form. There-is the-same greyness, the-same

violentia vultu,   oculi   lucent idem,
violence in-*his*-countenance, *his*-eyes glare the-same,

eadem   imāgo   feritātis.
there is the-same appearance of-ferocity.

The described shapeshifting of clothes into the hairs of the wolf, arms into legs, and wanting to speak but being unable is the first of its kind in recorded poetry. A thousand years later the poets of the Middle Ages continued the lycanthrope legend in their poetry.

One such early poem involving werewolves is "*Roman de Guillaume de Palerne*," which is thought to have been expounded from Italian legend in the late 1100s and translated to French in 1350 A.D. The poem was translated into modern English in 1832 from a rare copy of an ancient manuscript found in King's College Library of Cambridge and given the modern and endearing title: "William and the Werwolf."

In the 13th century a Frenchwoman known only as "Marie" gave us the poem now called "The Lay of Marie" or more properly, Marie's "Lai du Bisclavaret," which references the werewolf. A quote from the poem is given at the beginning of the short story "The Wehr-Wolf: A Legend of the Limousin."

Promulgation of the werewolf legend in Great Britain as it regards cattle and the devil is due in no small part to English poet Michael Drayton who penned "The Moon-Calf" in the late 16th century or early 17th century that tells of the fierce "wär-wolf" and its thirst for the blood of cattle.

A transformation of the werewolf in literature made its greatest strides in the 19th century when the monster leapt from poetry to the short story. It happened when this shorter form of literature was morphing into darker shapes thanks in no small part to Edgar Allan Poe, Honoré de Balzac, George Soane, E. T. A. Hoffmann, Nathaniel Hawthorne, Wilhelm Hauff, Charles Dickens, and Samuel Warren. Although each of these authors penned stories that are contained in "The Best Horror Short Stories 1800-1849" that I edited and introduced, you will surprisingly find none of them as authors of a werewolf short story in this collection. *Sigh.*

Only a few novels addressed werewolves in this time period. The first was "The Albigenses" published by Charles Maturin in 1824. This gothic novel, however, does not center around werewolves. A novella titled, "Norman of the Strong Arm: A Tale of the Sanctuary of Westminster," was penned by H. Laurence and published in 1827 in the Second Series of *London in the Olden Times*. It points out and draws upon the superstitions of the middle ages in many of the stories. In the last few pages of "Norman of the Strong Arm," a man is imprisoned for purportedly befriending a werewolf.

The first English novel in which a werewolf is the protagonist was serialized by George W. M. Reynolds in his *Reynold's Miscellany* from November 6, 1846 to July 24, 1847 and titled, "Wagner, the Wehr-Wolf." Reynolds was an author and editor of British Penny Dreadfuls that were very popular among the working classes during 1825-1855. These pulp rags contained mostly trash fiction, but in a few instances works that are remembered for being "first" in a particular genre. Two years later "Sidonia the Sorceress" was penned by Wilhelm Meinhold. It is a multi-volumed work that gives a fine example of a she-wolf.

Given the relative dearth of novels about werewolves leading up to and continuing through 1849, the appearance of werewolves in a number of short stories during this half-century is significant. The short story is not, as some believe, a lesser form of literature than the novel. Poe was quick to laud short fiction in his April 1842 review of "Twice Told Tales" in *Graham's Magazine*: "We have always regarded the *Tale* (using this word in its popular acceptation) as affording the best prose opportunity for display of the highest talent."

The fifty year period between 1800 and 1849 is truly the cradle of all werewolf short stories. Yet when this genre was in its infancy, this key period gave us some very good werewolf stories. One peculiar story that I did not include in this collection is "Ursel. The Water-Wolf" that was published in 1839, because it is unclear whether the water-wolf is a shapeshifted human. The only clue in the story is that wolves on the land howl when the creature approaches a boat from the water. The creature is never described in the story. A passage in Volume XXXV of *The Living Age* for 1881 provides some background in Germanic water tales and creatures:

Loki's name signifies the "flame" (Ger. *Lohe*) Nevertheless, he is the father both of the wolf Fenrir (the roarer from the deep), who is also called Wanargandr, that is, water-wolf, and of the midgard snake, which represents the world-encircling sea. From Fenrir's eyes and nose, fire glows; yet Fenrir, as the name proves, must originally have been a mythic being of the stormy waves. He is a water-wolf; but in old poems his name is also used as a synonym for fire. His progenitor, Loki, is said to have once lain, in monster shape, in the grove of hot springs. Albeit a fire-god, Loki is the "confidant of the whale." Under another name he is known as Loptr, that is, the Aërial, who dwells aloft; and this aërial character connects him with the waters of heaven. Freyja and Freyr, the offspring of a sea-god, are, in one of their aspects, typical solar deities. Their father, Niörd, who has a dwelling in Asgard, was said to be able to still both water and fire. Wate, the German watergiant, was the father of Wieland, or Wayland the Smith, a German Vulcan.

At the end of this anthology is a list of what short stories were considered in making this compilation along with the author and earliest publication date. Stories of rabid wolves were not considered in this collection.

Believing that the stories collected here truly are the finest werewolf stories for this half-century, they have been annotated for better understanding. If a particular story was annotated as published, those annotations are provided along with my annotations. In certain instances I have added dates and clarifications to the annotations as originally published to enhance the reading experience.

Please visit AndrewBarger.com for an exclusive interview regarding these stories as well as my blog:

www.scary-short-stories.blogspot.com to read my reviews of the best werewolf, horror, ghost and vampire short stories. As always, thanks for reading.

Andrew Barger
April 02, 2010

JAMES SUTHERLAND MENZIES
(1806-1883)

Φ

Hugues the Wer-Wolf
A Kentish Legend of the Middle Ages

The first of this collection is a classic werewolf story that has been widely reprinted. It was first published in the September 1838 issue of *The Court Magazine and Monthly Critic* by "S. M." The general belief is that the story was penned by Sutherland Menzies, although some believe it was really Elizabeth Stone writing under a penname (or penletters). The historical nature of this story and the detailed footnotes support Menzies as the author who later wrote such historical-based yawns as "Political Women" and "Royal Favorites."

Like a number of the short werewolf stories from 1800-1849, this tale is based in the middle ages and centers around the ancient Hugues family, as derived from the Norman extraction of Henry II, and its reputed lycanthropic bloodline. Menzies, in the second footnote of story, also informs us that Hugh Lupus was the first Earl Kent. A wolf's head was formed in his family crest.

"Hugues the Wer-Wolf" was not, however, the first werewolf short story to draw upon the legends surrounding this family or employ a protagonist named Hugues.

The name was used seven years earlier in "The Man-Wolf" by Leitch Ritchie. It is included in this collection for comparison.

The story before you is the first werewolf short story that involves the severing of a member. It also is the first to show that a werewolf's hide cannot be pierced by spear or arrow, though it is vulnerable to the edge of a steel blade.

"Hugues the Wer-Wolf" is set on All Souls' Eve, that haunted night of the year before All Souls' Day when the dead are reputed to rise from the graves and return to their homes. Before our modern Halloween, this was the most haunted night in all the year.

Hugues the Wer-Wolf
A Kentish Legend
of the Middle Ages

"Ye hallow'd bells, whose voices through the air
The awful summons of afflictions bear."

Honoria, on the Day of All Souls.

O N the confines of that extensive forest track formerly spreading over so large a portion of that garden of England, the lovely county of Kent, a remnant of which "woody way" to this day is known as the Weald of Kent,[1] and where it stretched its almost impervious covert midway between

---

[1] That silvan district, at the period to which our tale belongs, was an immense forest, desolate of inhabitants, and only occupied by wild swine and deer; and though it is now filled with towns and villages, and well peopled, the woods that remain sufficiently indicate its former extent. "And being at first," says Edward Hasted (1732-1812), "neither peopled nor cultivated, and only filled with herds of deer and droves of swine, belonged wholly to the king, for there is no mention of it but in royal grants and donations. And it may be presumed that, when the weald was first made to belong to certain known owners, as well as the rest of the country, it was not then allotted into tenancies, nor manured like the rest of it; but only as men were contented to inhabit it, and by piecemeal to clear it of the wood and convert it into tillage."— *Hasted's Kent,* vol. I., p. 134.

Ashford and Canterbury during the prolonged reign
of our second Henry, a family of Norman extraction,
by name Hugues—or Wulfric, as they were commonly
called by the Saxon inhabitants of that district—had,
under protection of the ancient forest laws, furtively
erected for themselves a lone and miserable
habitation; and amidst these sylvan fastnesses,
ostensibly following the occupation of wood-cutters,
the wretched outcasts—for such, for some cause or
other, they evidently were—had for many years
maintained a secluded and precarious existence.
Whether from rooted antipathy, actively cherished
against all that usurping nation from which these
woodmen derived their origin, or from recorded
malpractices, they had been long looked upon by
their superstitious Anglo-Saxon neighbours as
belonging to the accursed race of wer-wolves, and, as
such, churlishly refused work on the domains of the
surrounding franklins or proprietors; so thoroughly
was accredited the descent of the original
lycanthropic stain transmitted from father to son
through several generations.

That the Hugues Wulfrics reckoned not a single
friend among the adjacent huts and homesteads of
serf or freedman was not to be wondered at,
possessing, as they did, so formidable a reputation;
for to them was invariably attributed even the
misfortunes to which chance alone might seem to
have given birth. Did midnight fire consume the
grange; did the time-decayed barn, over-stored with
an unusually abundant harvest, tumble into ruins;
were the shocks of wheat laid prostrate over the
fields by tempest; did the smut destroy the grain, or
the cattle perish, decimated by murrain; a child sink
under some wasting malady, or a woman give
premature birth to her offspring, it was ever the
Hugues Wulfrics who were openly accused, eyed
aslant with mingled fear and detestation, the finger
of young and old pointing them out with bitter
execrations; in fine, they were almost as nearly

classed *feræ naturæ* as their fabled prototype, and dealt with accordingly.[2]

Terrible indeed were the tales told of them round the glowing hearth at eventide, whilst spinning the flax or plucking the geese; equally affirmed, too, in broad daylight, whilst driving the cows to pasturage; and most circumstantially discussed on Sundays, between mass and vespers, by the gossiping groups collected within Ashford church parvis,[3] with most seasonable admixture of anathema and devout crossings. Witchcraft, larceny, murder, and sacrilege, formed prominent features in the bloody and mysterious scenes of which the Hugues Wulfrics were the alleged actors. Sometimes they were ascribed to the father, at others to the mother; and even the daughter escaped not her share of vilification. Fain would they have attributed an atrocious disposition to the unweaned babe, so great, so universal was the horror in which was held that race of Cain!

The churchyard of Ashford, and the carved stone cross, from whence diverged the several roads to London, Canterbury, and Ashford, standing midway between the two last-named places, served—so tradition avouched—as nocturnal haunts for the unhallowed deeds of the Wulfrics, who thither prowled by moonlight, it was said, to fatten on the freshly buried dead, or drain the blood of any living wight who might be rash enough to venture near those solitary spots. True it was that the wolves had, during some of the severe winters, emerged from

---

[2] King Edgar (943-975) is said to have been the first who attempted to rid England of its wolves; criminals even being pardoned by producing a stated number of these creatures' tongues. Some centuries after, they increased to such a degree as to become again the object of royal attention, and Edward I. (1239-1307) appointed persons to extirpate this obnoxious race. It is one of the principal bearings in armory. Hugh, surnamed Lupus, (Hugh d'Avranches) the first Earl of Kent, bore for his crest a wolf's head.

[3] Courtyard in front of a church

their forest lairs, and entering the cemetery by a breach in its walls, goaded by famine, had actually disinterred the dead. True it was, also, that the Wolf's Cross, as the hinds commonly designated it, had been stained with gore on one occasion through the fall of a drunken mendicant, who chanced to fracture his skull against a pointed angle of its basement. But these accidents, as well as a multitude of others, were attributed to the guilty intervention of the Wulfrics, under their fiendish guise of wer-wolves.

These poor people, moreover, took no pains to exonerate themselves from a prejudice so monstrous. Full well aware of what calumny they were the victims, but alike conscious of their impotence to contradict it, they tacitly suffered its infliction, and fled all contact with those to whom they knew themselves repulsive. Shunning the highways, and never venturing to pass through the town of Ashford in open day, they pursued such labour as might occupy them within-doors or in unfrequented places. They appeared not at Canterbury market, never numbered themselves among the pilgrims at Becket's far-famed shrine, nor assisted at any sport, merry-making, hay-cutting, or harvest-home; the priest had interdicted them from all communion with the church—the ale-bibbers from the hostelry.

The rude hut which they inhabited was built of chalk and clay, with a thatch of straw, in which the high winds had made large rents; and its rotten door exhibited wide gaps, through which the wind had free ingress. As this wretched abode was situate at considerable distance from any other, if, perchance, any of the neighbouring serfs strayed within its precincts towards nightfall, their credulous fears made them shun near approach so soon as the vapours of the marsh were seen to blend their ghastly wreaths with the twilight. When that darkling time drew on which explains the diabolical sense of the old saying, "'tween dog and wolf," "'twixt hawk and buzzard," and the will-o'-the-wisps began to glimmer around the dwelling of the Wulfrics, they then patriarchally supped—whenever they had a supper,—and forthwith betook themselves to rest.

Sorrow, misery, and the putrid exhalations of the steeped hemp, from which they manufactured a rude and scanty attire, combined eventually to bring sickness and death into the bosom of this wretched family; who, in their utmost extremity, could hope for neither pity nor succour. The father was first attacked, and his corpse was scarce cold ere the mother rendered up her breath. Thus passed that fated couple to their account, unsolaced by the consolations of the confessor or the medicaments of the leech. Hugues Wulfric, their eldest son, himself dug their grave, laid their bodies within it, swathed with hempen shreds for grave clothes, and raised a few clods of earth over them, wherewith to mark their last resting-place. A hind, who chanced to see him fulfilling this pious duty in the dusk of the evening, timidly crossed himself, and fled as fast as his legs would carry him, fully believing that he had witnessed some infernal incantation. When the actual fact transpired, the neighbouring gossips congratulated one another upon the twofold mortality, which they looked upon as a tardy chastisement of Heaven. They spoke of ringing the joy bells, and offering masses of thanks for such a deed of grace.

It was All Souls' Eve, and the wind howled along the bleak hill-side, whistling drearily through the naked branches of the forest trees, whose last leaves it had remorselessly stripped; the sun had sunk obscurely; a dense and chilling fog spread through the air like the mourning veil of the widowed, whose day of love hath early fled. No star shone in the heavy, murky sky. In that lone hut, through which death had so lately passed, the orphan survivors held their lonely vigil by the fitful blaze sent forth from the reeking logs smouldering upon the hearth.

Several days had elapsed since their lips had pressed for the last time the cold hands of their parents; several dreary nights had passed since the sad hour in which their last farewell had left them desolate on earth.

Poor lone ones!—both, too, in the flower of their youth—how sad, yet how serene did they appear amid their grief! But what sudden and mysterious terror is it that seems to overcome them? It is not, alas! the first time since they were left alone upon earth, that they have found themselves at this hour of the night by their deserted hearth, once enlivened by the cheerful tales of their mother. Full often have they wept over her memory, but never yet had their solitude proved so appalling; and, pallid as very spectres, they tremblingly gazed upon one another as the flickering ray from the wood-fire played over their features.

"Brother! heard you not that loud shriek which every echo of the forest repeated? It sounds to me as if the ground were ringing with the tread of some gigantic phantom, and whose breath seems to have shaken the door of our hut. The breath of the dead they say is icy cold. A mortal shivering has come over me."

"And I too, sister, thought I heard voices as it were at a distance, murmuring strange words. Tremble not thus! Am I not beside you?"

"Oh, brother, let us pray the holy Virgin, to the end that she may restrain the departed from haunting our dwelling."

"But perhaps our mother is amongst them. She comes, unshrived and unshrouded, to visit her forlorn ones—her well-beloved! For knowest thou not, sister, 'tis the eve on which the dead forsake their graves? Let us open the door, that our mother may enter and resume her wonted place by the hearthstone."

"Oh, brother, how gloomy is all without doors! how damp and cold the gusts sweep by! Hearest thou what groans the dead are uttering round our hut? Oh, close the door, in Heaven's name!"

"Take courage, sister; I have thrown upon the fire that holy branch, plucked as it flowered on last Palm Sunday, which thou knowest will drive away all evil spirits; and now our mother can enter atone."

"But how will she look, brother? They say the dead are horrible to gaze upon; that their hair has fallen away, their eyes become hollow, and that in walking their bones rattle hideously. Will our mother, then, be thus?"

"No: she will appear with the features we loved to behold; with the affectionate smile that welcomed us home from our perilous labours; with the voice which, in early youth, sought us when, belated, the closing night surprised us far from our dwelling."

The poor girl busied herself awhile in arranging a few platters of scanty fare upon the tottering board which served them for a table; and this last pious offering of filial love, as she deemed it, appeared accomplished only by the greatest and last effort, so enfeebled had her frame become.

"Let our dearly loved mother enter, then," she exclaimed, sinking exhausted upon the settle. "I have prepared her evening meal, that she may not be angry with me; and all is arranged as she was wont to have it. But what ails thee, my brother? for now thou tremblest as I did awhile agone."

"Seest thou not, sister, those pale and lurid lights which are rising at a distance across the marsh? They are the dead, coming to seat themselves before the repast prepared for them. Hark! List to the funeral tones of the All-hallowtide bells, as they come upon the gale, blended with their hollow voices. Listen! listen!"

"Brother, this horror grows insupportable. This, I feel, of a verity, will be my last night upon earth! And is there no word of hope to cheer me, mingling with those fearful sounds? Oh, brother I brother!"

"Hush, sister, hush! Seest thou now the ghastly lights which herald the dead athwart the horizon? Hearest thou the prolonged tolling of the bell? They come! they come!"

"Eternal repose to their ashes!" exclaimed the bereaved ones, sinking upon their knees, and bowing down their heads in the extremity of their terror and lamentation; and as they uttered the words, the door was at the same moment closed with violence, as though it had been slammed to by a vigorous hand. Hugues started to his feet, for the cracking of the timber which supported the roof seemed to announce the fall of the frail tenement; the five was suddenly extinguished, and a plaintive groan mingled itself with the blast that whistled through the crevices of the door. On raising his sister, Hugues found that she too was no longer to be numbered among the living.

———

Hugues, on becoming the head of his family, composed of two sisters younger than himself, had seen them likewise descend into the grave in the space of a fortnight;[4] and when he had laid the last within her parent earth, he hesitated whether he should not extend himself beside them, and share their peaceful slumber. It was not by tears and sobs that grief so profound as his manifested itself, but in a mute and sullen contemplation over the rude sepulture of his kindred and his own future loneliness. During three consecutive nights he wandered, pale and haggard, from his solitary hut, to prostrate himself and kneel by turns upon the funereal turf. For three days food had not passed his lips.

Winter had interrupted the labours of the woods and fields, and Hugues had presented himself in vain

———

[4] Two weeks

among the neighbouring farms to obtain a few days' employment to thresh grain, cut wood, or drive the plough; no one would employ him, from fear of drawing upon himself the fatality attached to all bearing the name of Wulfric. He met with brutal denials at all hands; and not only were these accompanied by taunt and menace, but dogs were let loose upon him to rend his limbs; they deprived him even of the alms accorded to beggars by profession. In short, he found himself overwhelmed with scorn, insult, and injury.

Was he, then, to expire of inanition, or deliver himself from the tortures of hunger by suicide? He would have embraced that means, as a last and only consolation, had he not been retained earthward to struggle with his dark fate by a feeling of love. Yes, that abject being—forced, in very desperation against his better self, to abhor the human species in the abstract, and to feel a savage joy in waging war against it; that *pariah,* who scarce longer felt confidence in the Heaven which seemed an apathetic witness of his woes; that man, so isolated from those social relations which alone compensate us for the toils and troubles of life, without other stay than that afforded by his conscience, with no other fortune in prospect than the miserable existence and bitter death of his departed kin; worn to the bone by sorrow and privation, swelling with rage and resentment, he yet consented to live, to cling to life; for, strange to say, he loved! But for that heaven-sent ray gleaming across his thorny path, he would have gladly exchanged a pilgrimage so lone and wearisome for the peaceful slumber of the grave.

Hugues Wulfric would have been the finest youth in all that part of Kent, were it not that the outrages with which he had so unceasingly to contend, and the privations he was forced to undergo, had effaced the colour from his cheeks, and sunk his eyes deep in their orbits. His brows also were habitually contracted, and his glance oblique and fierce. Yet, despite that recklessness and anguish which clouded his features, one, incredulous of his alleged atrocities, could not have failed to admire the savage beauty of his head, cast in nature's noblest mould, crowned with a profusion of waving hair, and set upon shoulders whose robust and harmonious proportions were discoverable through the tattered attire investing them. With a carriage firm and majestic, his motions were not without a species of rustic grace, and the tone of his naturally soft voice accorded admirably with the purity in which he spoke his ancestral language—Norman French. In short, he differed so widely from people of his imputed condition, that one is constrained to believe that jealousy or prejudice must originally have been no stranger to the malicious persecution of which he was the object. The women alone ventured first to pity his forlorn condition, and next endeavoured to think of him in a more favourable light.

Branda, niece of Willieblud, the flesher[5] of Ashford, had, among other of the town maidens, noticed Hugues with a not unfavouring eye, as she chanced to pass one day on horseback through a coppice near the outskirts of the town, into which the young man had been led by the eager chase of wild hog; and which animal, from the nature of the country, was, single-handed, exceedingly difficult of capture. The cold-hearted falsehoods which the malignant crones buzzed in her ears in no wise diminished the advantageous opinion she had conceived of this ill-treated and good-looking wer-wolf. She sometimes, indeed, went so far as to turn considerably out of her way, in order to meet and exchange his cordial greeting; for Hugues, recognizing the attention of which he had now become the object, had, in his turn, at last summoned up courage to survey more leisurely the pretty Branda; and the result was that he found her the brightest and comeliest maiden

---

[5] Worker who removes flesh from the skin for making leather

that, in his hitherto restricted rambles out of the forest, his timorous gaze had ever encountered. His gratitude increased proportionally; and at the moment when his domestic bereavements came one after another to overwhelm him, he was actually on the eve of making Branda, on the first opportunity presenting itself, an avowal of the love he bore her.

It was chill winter—holy Christmas-tide; the distant toll of the curfew had long ceased, and all the inhabitants of Ashford were safely housed in their tenements for the night. Hugues—solitary, motionless, silent, his forehead grasped between his hands, his gaze dully fixed upon the decaying brands that feebly glimmered upon his hearth—heeded not the cutting north wind, whose sweeping gusts shook the crazy roof and whistled through the clunks of the door. He started not at the harsh cries of the herons fighting for prey in the marsh, nor at the monotonous croaking of the ravens perched over his smoke vent. He thought of his departed kindred, and imagined that his hour to rejoin them would soon be at hand; for the intense cold congealed the marrow of his bones, and fell hunger gnawed and twisted his entrails. Yet at intervals would a recollection of nascent love—of Branda—suddenly appease his else intolerable anguish, and cause a faint smile to gleam across his wan features.

"O blessed Virgin! grant that my sufferings may speedily cease!" murmured he, despairingly. "Oh, would I were a wer-wolf, as they call me! I could then requite them for all the foul wrong done me. True, I could not feed upon their flesh; I would not shed their blood; but I should be able to terrify and torment those who have wrought my parents' and sisters' death, who have persecuted our family even to extermination! Why have I not the power to change my nature into that of a wolf, if of a verity my ancestors possessed it, as they avouch? I should at least find carrion[6] to devour, and not die thus horribly of starvation. Branda is the only being in this world who cares for me; and that conviction alone reconciles me to life!"

Hugues gave free current to these gloomy reflections. The smouldering embers now gave but a feeble and vacillating light, faintly struggling with the surrounding gloom, and Hugues felt the horror of darkness coming strong upon him. Chilled with the ague fit one instant, and tormented the next by the fevered pulsation of his veins, he arose at last to seek some fuel, and threw upon the fire a heap of faggot chips, heath, and straw, which soon raised a clear and crackling flame. His stock of wood had become exhausted; and seeking wherewith to replenish his dying hearth-fire, whilst foraging under the rudely built oven, amongst a pile of rubbish placed there by his mother wherewith to bake bread,— handles of old tools, fractured joint-stools, and cracked platters,— he discovered a chest rudely bound with a dressed hide, and which he had never seen before. Rushing upon it as though he had found a treasure, he broke open the lid, strongly secured by an iron hasp.

This chest, which had evidently been long unopened, contained the complete disguise of a wer-wolf,—a dyed sheepskin, with gloves in the form of paws; a tail; a mask with an elongated muzzle, furnished with formidable rows of yellow horse-teeth.

Hugues started backwards, terrified at his discovery—so opportune that it seemed to him the work of sorcery. Then, on recovering from his surprise, he drew forth, one by one, the several pieces of this strange disguise, which had evidently seen some service, but from long neglect had become somewhat damaged. Then recurred confusedly to his mind the marvellous recitals made him by his grandfather, as he nursed him upon his knees

---

[6] Horse-flesh was an article of food among our Saxon forefathers in England.

during earliest childhood,—tales during the narration of which his mother wept silently, as he had laughed heartily. In his mind there was a mingled strife of feelings and purposes alike indefinable. He continued his examination of this criminal heritage, and by degrees his imagination grew bewildered with vague and extravagant projects.

Hunger and despair together hurried him on. He saw objects no longer save through an ensanguined prism. He felt his very teeth on edge with an avidity for biting. He experienced an inconceivable impulse to run. He set himself to howl, as though he had practised wer-wolfery all his life, and next began to invest himself completely with the guise and external attributes of his novel vocation. A more startling change could scarcely have been wrought in him had that horribly grotesque metamorphosis really been the effect of enchantment; aided too, as it was, by the fever which worked a temporary insanity in his frenzied brain.

Scarcely did he thus find himself travestied into a wer-wolf through the influence of his shaggy vesture, ere he darted forth from the hut, through the forest and into the open country—white with hoar-frost, and across which the bitter north-east wind swept—howling in a frightful manner, and traversing the meadows, fallows, plains, and marshes, like a phantom. But at that hour, and during such a season, not a single belated wayfarer was there to encounter Hugues, whom the keenness of the air and the excitation of his run had worked up to the highest pitch of extravagance and audacity. He howled the louder in proportion as his hunger waxed sharper.

Suddenly the heavy rumbling of an approaching vehicle arrested his attention. At first with indecision, next with a stolid fixity of purpose, he struggled with two suggestions counseling him at one and the same moment—to flee and to advance. The carriage, or whatever it might be, continued rolling towards him. The night was not so obscure but that he was able to descry the tower of Ashford Church at a short distance off, and hard by which stood a pile of unhewn stone, destined either for the execution of some repair, or addition to the sacred edifice, into the deep shadow of which he ran furtively to crouch down, and so await the coming up of his prey.

It proved to be the covered cart of Willieblud, the Ashford flesher, who was wont twice a week to carry meat to Canterbury, and travelled by night in order that he might be among the first at market opening. Of this Hugues was fully aware, and the departure of the flesher naturally suggested to him the inference that his niece must be keeping house by herself—for our lusty flesher had been long a widower. For an instant he hesitated whether he should introduce himself, thus strangely accoutered, to the maiden— favourable as the opportunity seemed,—or whether he should first attack the uncle and seize upon his viands. Hunger, for the nonce, got the better of love; and the monotonous whistle with which the driver was, as usual, urging forward his sorry jade, warning him to be in readiness for his onset, he suddenly howled in a loud and unearthly tone, at the same moment that he rushed forwards and seized the horse by the bit. " Willieblud, flesher!" growled Hugues, disguising his voice, and speaking to him in the *lingua Franca* of that period, "I hunger; throw me two pounds of meat if thou wouldst live and have me live."

"St. Winifred have mercy upon me!" cried the terrified flesher; "is it thou, Hugues Wulfric, of Weald Marsh, the born wer-wolf?"

"Thou sayest sooth; it is I," replied Hugues, who had the ready address to avail himself of the credulous superstition of Willieblud. "I would rather have raw beef than eat of thy flesh, plump as thou art. Throw me, therefore, what I crave, and forget not to be ready with a like portion each time thou settest out for Canterbury market; or, failing thereof, I'll tear thee limb from limb."

Hugues, to display his attributes of a wer-wolf before the gaze of the terrified flesher, had sprung upon the spokes of the wheel, and placed his fore-paw upon the edge of the cart, over which he made a semblance of snuffing with his false snout. Willieblud, who believed in wolves as devoutly as he did in his patron saint, had no sooner perceived this monstrous paw than, uttering a fervent invocation to the latter, he seized upon his daintiest joint of meat, let it fall to the ground, and whilst Hugues sprung eagerly down to pick it up, the flesher at the same instant dealt a sudden and sharp blow on his beast's flank, on which the latter set off at a sharp gallop without waiting for any reiterated invitation from the lash.

Hugues, satiated with a repast which had cost him far less trouble to procure than any he had long remembered, readily promised himself the renewal of an expedient the execution of which was at once so easy and diverting; for, though smitten with the charms of the fair-haired Branda, he not the less found a malicious pleasure in augmenting the terror of her uncle Willieblud. The latter, for a long while, revealed not to living being the tale of his late encounter and strange compact with Hugues, but submitted unmurmuringly to the impost levied each time the wer-wolf crossed his path, without being very nice about either weight or quality of the meat. He no longer even waited to be asked for it;— anything rather than encounter that fiend-like form clinging to the side of his cart, or being brought into close contact with that hideous, misshapen paw, stretched forth, as it were, to strangle him,—that paw, too, which once had been a human hand. The flesher, moreover, had become moody and morose of late; he set out to market reluctantly, and seemed to dread the hour of departure as it drew nigh, and no longer beguiled the dullness of his nocturnal journey by whistling to his horse, or by trolling snatches of ballads, as he was wont formerly. Willieblud now invariably returned home in a gloomy and restless mood.

Branda, at a loss to conceive what had given rise to this new and permanent depression that had taken hold of her uncle's mind, after in vain exhausting conjecture, proceeded to interrogate, importune, and supplicate him by turns; until the unhappy flesher, no longer proof against such continuous appeals, at last disburdened himself of the load which he had at heart, by recounting the history of his nocturnal adventures with the wer-wolf.

The quick-witted Branda listened demurely and patiently to the entire story without offering either comment or query. At its close,—

"Hugues is no more a wer-wolf than thou art!" exclaimed she, hurt that such an injurious suspicion should be entertained against one for whom she had long felt something more than interest. "'Tis an idle tale, or some juggling device. I fear me thou must of a verity dream these sorceries, uncle Willieblud; for Hugues, of the Weald Marsh, or Wulfric, as the silly fools call him, is worth far more, I trow, than his reputation goes."

"Girl, it boots not saying me nay in this matter," replied Willieblud, pertinaciously urging the truth of his story. "The family of Hugues, as everybody knows, were wer-wolves born; and since they are all of late, by the blessing of Heaven, defunct, save one,—Hugues himself now, of a verity, inherits the wolfs paw."

"I tell thee, and will avouch it openly, uncle, that Hugues is of too gentle and seemly a nature to serve Satan, and turn himself into a wild beast, and that will I never believe until I have seen the same."

"Mass! and that thou shalt right speedily, if thou wilt but along with me. In very sooth, 'tis he. Besides, when he made confession of his name, did I not recognize his voice? and am I not ever bethinking me of his knavish paw, with which he grasps the cart shaft while he stays the horse? Girl, mark me, he is in league with the foul fiend."

Branda had to a certain degree imbibed the lycanthropic superstition in the abstract, as well as her uncle; saving, so far as it concerned the hitherto, as she believed, traduced being on whom her affections, as though in feminine perversity, had so strangely lighted: Her womanish curiosity, in this instance, less determined her resolution to accompany the flesher on his next journey, than the desire to exculpate her lover,—fully believing the strange tale of her kinsman's encounter with and spoliation by the latter to be the effect of some strange illusion, and of which to find Hugues guilty was the sole dread she experienced on mounting the rude vehicle laden with its customary viands.

It was just midnight when they started from Ashford, the hour alike dear to wer-wolves as to goblins of every other denomination. Hugues was punctual at the appointed spot. His howlings, as they drew nigh, though horrible enough, had still something human in them, and disconcerted not a little the confidence of Branda. Willieblud, however, trembled even more than she did, and sought for the wolf's portion; the latter raised himself upon his hind legs, and extended one of his forepaws to receive the mulctuary dole as soon as the cart stopped at the heap of stones.

"Uncle, I shall swoon with affright," exclaimed Branda, clinging closely to the flesher, and tremblingly pulling the coverchief over her eyes; "loose rein and smite thy beast, or evil will surely betide us."

"Thou art not alone, gossip," cried Hugues, fearful of a snare; "if thou essay'st to play me false, certes thou'rt at once undone."

"Harm us not, friend Hugues, thou know'st I weigh not my pounds of meat with thee; I shall take heed to keep my troth. It is Branda, my niece, who goes with me to-night to buy wares at Canterbury."

"Branda with thee? By the mass 'tis she indeed, more buxom and rosy, too, than ever; come, pretty one, descend and tarry awhile, that I may have speech with thee."

"I conjure thee, good Hugues, terrify not so cruelly my poor wench, who is well-nigh dead already with fear; suffer us to hold our way, for we have far to go, and to-morrow is early market-day."

"Go thy ways then alone, Uncle Willieblud; 'tis thy niece I would have speech with, in all courtesy and honour; the which, if thou permittest not readily and of a good grace, I will rend thee both to death."

All in vain was it that Willieblud exhausted himself in prayers and lamentation, in hopes of softening the bloodthirsty wer-wolf, as he believed him to be,— refusing as the latter did every sort of compromise in avoidance of his demand, and at last replying only by horrible threats, which froze the hearts of both. Branda, although especially interested in the debate, neither stirred foot nor opened her mouth, so greatly had terror and surprise overwhelmed her. She kept her eyes fixed upon the wer-wolf, who peered at her likewise through his mask, and felt incapable of offering resistance, when she found herself forcibly dragged out of the cart, and deposited, as it seemed to her, by an invisible power, beside the heap of stones. She swooned without uttering a single scream.

The flesher was no less dumbfounded at the turn the adventure had taken; and he too fell back among his meat, as though stricken by a blinding blow. He fancied that the wolf had swept his bushy tail violently across his eyes, and on recovering the use of his senses, found himself alone in the cart, which was rolling along joltingly at a rapid pace towards Canterbury. At first he listened, but in vain, for the wind to bring him either the shrieks of his niece, or the howlings of the wolf; but stop his beast he could not, which, panic-stricken, kept tearing on as though bewitched, or that she felt the spur of some fiend pricking her flanks.

Willieblud, however, reached his journey's end in safety, sold his meat, and returned to Ashford; reckoning full sure upon having to say a *miserere*[7] for his niece, whose fate he had not ceased to bemoan during the whole way. But how great was his astonishment to find her safe at home, a little pale from her recent fright and want of sleep, but without even a scratch. Still more was he astonished to hear that the wer-wolf had done her no injury whatever; contenting himself, after she had recovered from her swoon, with conducting her back to their dwelling, and acting in every respect like a loyal suitor, rather than a sanguinary wer-wolf. Willieblud knew not what to think of it.

This nocturnal gallantry towards his niece had additionally irritated the burly Saxon against the wer-wolf; and although the fear of reprisals kept him from making a direct and public attack upon Hugues, he ruminated not the less upon taking some sure and secret revenge. But previous to putting his design into execution, it struck him that he could not do better than relate his misadventure to the ancient sacristan and parish gravedigger of St. Michael's—a worthy of profound sagacity in those matters, who being, moreover, endowed with a clerk-like erudition, was consulted as an oracle in *glamour* by all the old crones and lovelorn maidens throughout the township of Ashford and its vicinity.

"Slay a wer-wolf thou canst not," was the repeated rejoinder of the wiseacre to the earnest inquiries of the tormented flesher; "for his hide is proof against spear or arrow, though vulnerable to the edge of a cutting weapon of steel. I counsel thee to deal him a slight flesh wound, or cut him over the paw, in order to know of a surety whether it be Hugues or no.

---

[7] A defined prayer for mercy

Thou'lt run no danger, save thou strikest him a blow from which blood flows not therefrom; for so soon as his skin is severed he taketh flight."

Resolving to follow implicitly the sacristan's advice, Willieblud that same evening determined to know with what sort of wer-wolf he had to do; and with that view hid his cleaver, newly sharpened for the occasion, under the meat in his cart; and held himself ready to make good use of it, as a preparatory step towards identifying Hugues as the audacious spoliator of his meat, and eke his peace. The wolf-man on this occasion presented himself as usual, and anxiously inquired after Branda, which stimulated the flesher the more firmly to follow out his design.

"Here, wolf," said Willieblud, stooping over the cart as if to choose a piece of meat; "I give thee double portion to-night. Up with thy paw, take toll, and be mindful of my frank alms."

"In sooth I will remember thee, gossip," rejoined our wer-wolf; "but when shall the marriage be solemnized for certain 'twixt me and the pretty Branda?".

Hugues believing he had nothing to fear from the flesher, whose meats it was his wont so illicitly to appropriate to himself, and of whose fair niece he hoped also to take shortly lawful possession—both that he really loved her, and viewed his union with her as the surest means of replacing him within the pale of that sociality from which he had been so long and so unjustly exiled, could he but succeed in making intercession with the holy fathers of the church so far as to obtain a removal of their interdict,—Hugues, as usual, placed his expectant paw upon the edge of the cart; whereupon, instead of handing him his joint of beef or mutton, Willieblud raised his cleaver, and, at a single blow, lopped off the member laid there as fittingly for the purpose as though upon a block. Having dealt the blow, the flesher flung down his weapon and belaboured his beast; at the same time the maimed wer-wolf howled aloud with agony, and then disappeared like a phantom amongst the dark shades of the forest, in which, aided by the wind, his howls and moans were soon lost to the ear.

The flesher, on his return home next day, chuckling and laughing, deposited a gory cloth upon the table among the trenchers with which his niece was busied in preparation of their noontide meal, and which wrapper, on being unfolded, displayed to her terrified gaze a freshly severed human hand, enveloped in a wolfskin glove. Branda, intuitively guessing what had happened, shrieked aloud, shed a flood of tears, and then hurriedly threw her mantle around her, whilst her uncle was amusing himself by turning and twitching about the lopped hand with a ferocious delight, exclaiming, as he wiped up the blood which still flowed from it,—

"The sacristan said sooth; the wer-wolf hath his meed, I trow, at last. And now I wot of his nature, I fear no further his witchcraft."

Although the day was far advanced, Hugues lay writhing in torture upon his wretched couch, his habiliments drenched with gore, as was also the floor of his hut. His visage, of a ghastly pallor, expressed as much moral as physical suffering. Tears gushed at intervals from beneath his red and swollen eyelids, and he listened to every sound without doors with an increasing inquietude, painfully visible upon his distorted features. At last he distinguished footsteps rapidly approaching his dismal abode; the door was hastily flung open, and, to his surprise, a female knelt beside his couch, and with mingled sobs and imprecations sought tenderly for his mutilated wrist, which, rudely swathed in hempen wrappings, no longer strove to conceal the absence of its hand, and from which a crimson stream still trickled. At so piteous a sight the tender-hearted maiden grew loud in her denunciations of the sanguinary flesher, and sympathetically mingled her lamentations with those of his victim.

These effusions of love and grief, however, were doomed to sudden interruption. Some one knocked at the shattered door of the wretched abode. Branda sprang to the loophole which served for a window, in order that she might see who the visitor might be that had dared to penetrate to the lair of a wer-wolf, and on recognizing him, raised her hands and eyes towards heaven in silent token of the extremity of her despair, while the knocking momentarily grew louder and louder.

"'Tis my uncle," she whispered, in faltering accents. "Ah! woe's me! how shall I escape hence without his seeing me?—whither hide? Oh, here, here, nigh to-thee, Hugues, and we will die together;" and she crouched herself down in a dark recess behind his couch. "Should Willieblud raise his cleaver to slay thee, he shall first strike through thy Branda's body."

So saying, she hastily hid her pretty little form amongst a pile of undressed hemp, at the same time whispering Hugues to summon all his courage; who, poor fellow, scarce found strength enough to raise himself to a sitting posture, whilst his languid gaze vainly sought around for some weapon of defence.

"A good day to thee, Wulfric!" sneered Willieblud, as he stepped into the hut, holding in his hand a cloth folded and tied in a knot, which he flung down upon an old coffer standing beside the wounded man; "I come to proffer thee work, knowing that thou art no laggard at billhook[8] and wattle.[9] Wilt bind and stack me a faggot pile? Wilt do it, I say?"

"I am sick," replied Hugues, repressing the bitter wrath he felt at heart, and which, despite the physical suffering he was undergoing, flashed in his

---

[8] European tool for cutting wood
[9] Mesh of sticks

wild and haggard glances, "I am not in fitting trim for work."

"Sick, gossip—sick art thou, indeed? Or is it only a sloth fit? Come, come, what ails thee? Let us see where lieth the malady. Your hand, that I may feel how beateth thy pulse."

Hugues' pallid cheek reddened, and for an instant he hesitated whether he should resist a solicitation, the object of which he too readily comprehended; but in order to avoid exposing the tender-hearted damsel to her uncle's discovery, the maimed lover thrust forth his left hand from beneath the coverture, all imbrued with dried gore.

"Not that hand, Hugues; let's have the other—the right one. Body o' me, man, hast lost thy fist, and must I find it for thee?"

Hugues, whose flush of rage had alternately deepened and turned to a deathlike hue, replied not to this taunt, nor testified by the slightest gesture or movement that he was about to comply with a request as cruel in the nature of its preconcertion as the object of it was slenderly cloaked. Willieblud laughed with a loud, coarse laugh, and ground his great teeth together in savage glee, maliciously reveling in the mental torture he saw clearly he was now inflicting upon the sufferer. He seemed disposed to use violence rather than allow himself to be baffled in the attainment of the decisive proof he aimed at. Already had he commenced untying the napkin, giving vent all the while to a string of pitiless taunts—one hand only displaying itself outside the coverture, and which Hugues, well-nigh senseless with anguish, thought not of withdrawing.

"Why tender me that hand?" continued his unrelenting persecutor, as he imagined himself on the eve of arriving at the conviction he so persistently sought for,—"that I should lop it off? Quick! quick! Master Wulfric, and do my bidding! I demand to see your right hand."

"Behold it then!" ejaculated a feigned voice, which belonged to no supernatural being, however it might seem appertaining to such; and Willieblud, to his utter confusion and dismay, saw a right hand, sound and unmutilated, extend itself towards him, as though in silent accusation. He started back, stammered out a cry for mercy, bent his knees for an instant, and then raising himself, palsied with terror, fled from the hut, which he firmly believed to be in the possession of the foul fiend. So great was his terror and consternation, that he left behind him the severed hand, which from that moment became a perpetual vision ever present before his bewildered mind, and which all the potent exorcisms of the sacristan, at whose hands he continually sought counsel and consolation, signally failed to dispel.

"Oh that hand! To whom, then, belongs that accursed hand?" groaned Willieblud, despondingly. "Is it really the fiend's, or that of some wer-wolf? Certain 'tis that Hugues is innocent, for did I not see both his hands? But wherefore was one all bloody? There's sorcery at the bottom of it, nathless!"

The next morning early, the first object that struck his sight on entering his stall was the severed hand that he had left the preceding night upon the coffer in the forest hut. It was stripped of its wolfskin glove, and lay all gaunt and livid among the flesher's viands. Such was his trepidation at the spectacle that he no longer dare touch the phantom hand, which now he verily believed to be enchanted; but, hoping to get rid of it at once and for ever, he had it flung into a well; and it was with no slight increase of perturbation that he found it shortly afterwards lying exposed upon his block in the vending booth. He next buried it in his garden, but still without being able to rid himself of the haunting apparition. It returned more livid and loathsome than ever to infect his shop, and augment the remorse which was unceasingly revived by the reproaches of his niece.

At length, flattering himself with the hope of escaping all further persecution from that fatal hand, it struck him that he would have it carried to the cemetery at Canterbury, and try whether solemn exorcism and sepulture in consecrated ground would bar effectually its return to the air and light of day. This was duly done. But lo! on the following morning, to his horror and mortification, he perceived it nailed to his shutter. Disheartened thoroughly by these dumb though awful reproaches, which entirely robbed him of his peace, and impatient to annihilate all trace of an action with which Heaven itself seemed to upbraid him, he quitted Ashford one morning without bidding adieu even to his niece, and some days after was found drowned in the river Stour. They drew out his swollen and discoloured body, which had been discovered floating on the surface among the sedge, and it was only by piecemeal that they succeeded in tearing away from his death-contracted clutch the phantom hand, which, in his suicidal convulsions, he had retained rigidly grasped.

A year after this event Hugues Wulfric, although *minus* a hand, and therefore a confirmed wer-wolf, married the pretty Branda, his faithful leman, and sole heiress to the stock and chattels of her uncle, the late unhappy flesher of Ashford.[10]

---

[10] Lycanthropy—which the foregoing tale attempts to illustrate—is a superstition of very remote antiquity, and has long been involved in much obscurity. It pervaded Greece, Rome, and the Germanic nations, and in all probability came down to them from the Chaldeans and those nomadic people who had unceasingly to defend their flocks from the attacks of wolves. The terror that those ferocious beasts spread by prowling at night round the fold proved favourable to malefactors, who, assuming the guise of furious wolves, were the better enabled to perpetrate acts of theft or vengeance. Hence seems to have been derived a superstition which has prevailed through all ages and nations under different names, and surrounded by circumstances and features more or less strange. Lucian (125-180) and Pliny (23-79), among the pagans, as well as the ghostly councils and the skilful leeches of the Middle Ages, busied themselves by turns with the lycanthropes, alike

in cursing, excommunicating, and curing them. When Gervoise of Tilbury (1150-1228) flourished (in the reigns of Henry II. and Richard I.), the extirpation of British wolves was very far from being complete, so that strong vestiges of this superstition were yet in our island. "We have frequently seen," he says, "men in England transformed into wolves for the space of a lunar month, and such people are called gerulphs *(garoux)* by the French, and wer-wolves by the English." Camden, in his notice of the county of Tipperary, says they have "a report of men turned every year into wolves," but adds that he accounts it fabulous.

Wer-wolf *(man-wolf)* is supposed to be an exact equivalent to the Greek word *lycanthropus,—were* being, in Anglo-Saxon, a man; whence some derive the *were-gild,* or composition money paid for homicide.

LEITCH RITCHIE
(1800-1865)

Φ

The Man-Wolf

I am unable to find the following tale of the werewolf previously collected in any anthology. It first appeared in 1831 and was penned by Leitch Ritchie in his two volume collection titled: "The Romance of History: France." The stories contained within it are what we today term historical fiction. The political narrative and characters stem from Robert le Pieux and Henry I; the later of which gives us the name Hugues. It is from the Norman extraction as it related to the royal family. The tale is set in the early 11th century during the reign of Henry I and is the first werewolf short story to have a protagonist named Hugues.

Though little read now, Leitch Ritchie was popular in his day. He wrote other short story collections like "The Romance of History: Spain," "The Tale Book," and "Winter Evenings."

Through his scholarship Ritchie has given us the first English werewolf short story to involve a monk, knight, and of course, a man named Hugues. It is the longest story of this collection and the second oldest. It will keep you guessing until the very end.

The Man-Wolf

Oh, flesh, flesh, how art thou finished!
Shakespeare.

JE ME SOUVIENS, EN EFFET, QU' À LA TABLE DU SÉNÉSCHAL ÉTAIT UN SEIGNEUR QUI FAISAIT RIRE LES CONVIVES PAR LA MANIÈRE GAUCHE AVEC LAQUELLE IL MANIAIT LA FOURCHETTE ET LES COUTEAUX; MAIS COMMENT ME SERAIS-JE IMAGINÉ QUE JE SOUPAIS AVEC UN ANCIENT LOUP?[1]–TRISTAN LE VOYAGEUR.[2]

IT WAS the third day after the grand procession in honour of Saint Ursula and the other virgin martyrs,[3] and yet the town of Josselin was far

---

[1] I remember, in fact, that at the table Sénéschal was a lord who was laughing with the guests about the manner with which he wielded the knife and fork, but would I be, as I imagined, the soup of an ancient wolf?

[2] French quote from "Tristan le Voyageur, ou la France au XIV Siecle, Louis-Antoine-François de Marchangy (1782-1826), Six Volumes, 1825-1826.

[3] The martyrdom of the eleven thousand Virgins is placed by some writers about the end of the fourth century. When Conan, say they, with eleven thousand British warriors, in the service of the emperor Magnus Maximus (335-388), (or of Constantine, Tyran.) conquered Armorica, and founded the kingdom of Little Britain, or Brittany, the emperor, to reward his valour, sent to demand from Dionotus (fictional person), King of Cornwall, as many virgins as would suffice to wive the whole body. Dionotus, accordingly, despatched his daughter Ursula and eleven thousand of the *éhte* of the British virginity in this laudable

from having returned to its wonted repose. The bells of Notre Dame du Roncier still rang out every now and then, as if forgetting that the fete was over; crowds were seen rolling, and meeting, and breaking in the streets; banners floated from the windows, and flowers and branches tapestried the walls. The representatives, indeed, of the eleven thousand Virgins had begun to disappear from the gaze of an equivocal worship, like the flowers at the close of summer. Every hour some glittering fragment was seen detaching itself from the mass, and as the beautiful pensionnaire,[4] in her litter, or on her palfrey, raised her head sidelong to listen to the discourse of some wandering knight, whom chance, or our Lady of the Bramble-bush,[5] had bestowed on her for an escort, she might have been observed to throw forwards into the distance a glance of fear, or at least distaste, to where the bars of her monastic cage seemed to gape for their accustomed prisoner. The ladies of the neighbourhood too, and the high-born cameristes of the nobility, as they floated homewards, surrounded by the chivalry of their province, sighed heavily when the towers of the

---

enterprise; but the fair adventurers being cast on shore by a tempest among the Huns and Picts, and declining to receive their hands in substitution for those of their own countrymen, were mercilessly sent to heaven by the ruffians with the double crown of virginity and martyrdom. This story has puzzled every body but those of the learned society of Sorbonne, who chose Saint Ursula (fictional person) for their patroness. Cornwall is no doubt better peopled now than it was then; and if it possesses to-day eleven thousand handsome and marriageable virgins, all that can be said is, that it is a great shame.

[4] Lady who pays a pension for room and board

[5] Roncier; so denominated because her statue was found buried among brambles. This simulacrum, by the way, has been supposed to be the property of Isis, or at least of the Roman Lares and Penates. —Ogée, "Dict. de Bret." The pious fraud is not uncommon; even Venus sometimes has been transubstantiated into the Holy Virgin.— Martin, "Religion du Gaulois."

chateau of the house of Porhoet[6] melted away in the golden sky; and the humbler damsels of the villages, to whom a part in the procession had been accorded, from the difficulty of finding so many virgins of high rank, waved mournfully their chaplets of blue-bells in token of adieu, and as the evening drew in, looked round in terror for the wandering fires of the sotray, and the dwarfs who dance at night round the peulvan.

A sufficient number still remained, however, to give an appearance of bustle and animation to the town; and it was thought that so great a concourse had never before been known to grace the annual ceremony of ducking the fishermen,[7] which took place on the day when this history commences. The crowd which lined the river-side was immense. Ladies, knights, and squires, chatelaines of the neighbourhood, priests, bourgeois and villeins—all were jumbled together with as little distinction as it was possible for the feudal pact to sanction. Minstrels, trouveres, and jongleurs mingled in the crowd, some singing, some striking the cymbals, and some reciting stories. Tables were spread in the midst where savoury viands were eagerly bought by the spectators,—for it was now more than two hours since dinner, being past midday. Instead of tablecloths, the ancient economical substitute of flowers and leaves was tastefully arranged upon the board, and streams of wine and hippocras played from naked statues, in a manner which in our lime would be reckoned less delicate than ingenious.

The bells at last began to ring, and the trumpets to bray; and the judges of the place, surrounded with banners, and all the pride, pomp, and circumstance of authority, entered upon the scene. Having taken their station, a solemn proclamation was made, calling upon all the persons who had sold, during

---

[6] Afterward possessed by the celebrated Olivier de Clisson (1326-1407)
[7] Ogée, t. 2, p. 204

Lent, fish taken in the river, to compeer then and there, either personally or by proxy, and for the satisfaction of the lieges,[8] and in token of fealty and submission to the lord of the fief, to throw a somerset in the said river, under pain of a fine of three livres and four sous.

A simultaneous shout arose from the multitude when the crier finished, and the air was shaken for many minutes by a burst of laughter like the neighing of a whole nation of Houyhnhnms.[9] One by one, the fish-merchants answered to the summons; some defying the ridicule of their situation by an air of good-humoured audacity; some looking solemn and sulky; and some casting a glance of marked hostility upon the turbulent and rapid waters before them. These feudal victims, generally speaking, were stout young fellows; but a few among them were evidently quiet townsfolk, who had nothing to do with the catching of the fish they had had the misfortune to sell.

Two or three appeared to be the rustic retainers of gentlemen who had not scrupled to make profitable use of the river where it watered their estates, but who were altogether disinclined to do homage in their own persons; and these *locum tenentes*[10] more especially looked with extreme disgust upon an element with which they were connected neither by habit nor interest. Owing to the late rains, indeed, the stream on this day presented an appearance, not very inviting to the unpractised bather. The black and swollen waters came down with a sullen turbulence, and an eddy whirling violently in the deep pool chosen for the scene of the divers' exploits, was somewhat startling to the imagination. Some were followed to the water's edge by the elder women of their families visiting and encouraging them, and

---

[8] Person owing allegiance to a feudal lord
[9] Race of smart horses that ruled over people in "Gulliver's Travels" by Jonathan Swift (1667-1745)
[10] Placeholders

others were egged on to the adventure by the sheathed swords of their masters, who seemed to enter into the joke with great gusto, shouting and clapping their hands at every deeper plunge.

The sport at length suffered some interruption from the backwardness of a country fellow, whose master in vain endeavoured, partly by fair words and partly by punches with the hilt of his sword, to drive him into the river.

"For the love of the Virgin," said the recusant, "only look at these black and muddy waters! It was on this very spot I saw last Easter the Leader of Wolves step grimly upon the bank in the moonlight, followed by his hellish pack; and, now I think on't, if he did not look at me fixedly with his dead eye, I am no Christian man, but a heathen Turk!"

"Thou shalt tell me the story again—thou shalt indeed," said the master, a man in the prime of life, and a knight by his golden spurs,—"but in with thee now, good Hugues,—in with thee, for the honour of the house! 'Tis but a step—a jump—a plunge; thou wilt float, I'll warrant thee, like a duck. Now, shut thy mouth, wink thine eyes, and leap, in the name of Saint Gildas!"[11]

"Saint Gildas, indeed!" said the man,—"I am neither a duck nor a saint, I trow. I cannot roost upon the waters, not I, with my legs gathered up into my doublet. Were it a league to the bottom, I should down. Neither can I tuck the waves under me like a garment, and sail away in the fashion of the Abbot of Rhuys, as light as a fly in a cockle-shell, singing, *Deus, in adjutorium!*"[12]

---

[11] Abelard was a successor of this saint in the abbacy of the monastery at Rhuys, where the pulpit of the lover of Heloise is still shown to the visiter.

[12] The Devil, intending to play St. Gildas (516-570) a trick, sent four of his confidential spirits, disguised as monks, to beseech him to repair with them to the convent of St. Philibert, where a friend *in articulo mortis* desired to see him. The saint, although knowing well enough what lurked under the cowl, embarked with the false monks; but the

"Want of faith, good Hugues," returned the knight, repressing his vexation,—"nothing save want of faith." But as the crowd began to murmur aloud, his choler awoke, and with a vigorous arm he dragged the victim to the water's edge.

"Beast that thou art!" he exclaimed, "shall the honour of the house of Keridreux be stained by a blot like thee? In with thee, rebellious cur,[13] or I will pitch thee into the middle of the stream like a clod!"[14]

"I will then," said the man, with a gasp, "I will indeed. Holy Saints, I had ever such an aversion to water! For the love of the Virgin, just give me a push, as if by accident, for my legs feel as if they were growing from the bank. Stay—only one moment! Wait till I have shut my eyes and my mouth. I will make as if I was looking into the river, and the bystanders will think we have been discoursing of the fish."

The Knight clenched his hand in a fury, as the murmurs of the crowd rose into a shout; and while Hugues was running over the names of as many saints as he could remember in so trying a moment—Notre Dame du Roncier, Saint Yves, Saint Brieuc, Saint Gildas,—he lent him a blow that would assuredly have sent him beyond the middle of the stream, had not the Tictim, moved either by a presentiment of danger, or by some sudden qualm of cowardice, sprung round at the same instant, and caught, as if with a death-grip, by his master's doublet. The force which he had exerted almost sufficed of itself to overbalance the knight, and it is no wonder, therefore, that the next moment both master and man were floundering in the river.

A rush took place to the water's edge at this novel exhibition. The bourgeois clapped their hands and

---

party was no sooner fairly out to sea, than he began to chant with a loud voice, *Deus, in adjutorium!* when the boat immediately went to pieces, the demons disappeared, and he himself was carried respectfully by the waves to land.

[13] Mutt

[14] Wad or compact mass

shouted to the depth of their throats; the ladies screamed; and those who had handsome knights near them fainted; all was noise and confusion among the crowd.

The knight, in the mean time, being tall, had gained a footing, although up to his neck in water; where he stood tugging at his sword, and casting round a bloodthirsty glance, resolving to sacrifice the caitiff who had so villainously compromised the dignity of the house of Keridreux, before emerging from the river. Hugues was carried out of his reach by the current, and dragged on shore amid the jeers of the bystanders; and the stout knight, as soon as he had become aware of this fact, rejecting indignantly the assistance that was offered him, climbed up on the bank, and clearing a space with a single circle of his sword, strode up to his intended victim. Another instant would have decided the fate of Hugues, who, having escaped a watery death, seemed to view with composure the perils of the land; but a lady, breaking through the circle of spectators, stepped in between him and his master.

"A boon! a boon! Sir Knight," she exclaimed; "give me the villain's life, for the honour of chivalry!" The Sire of Keridreux started back as if at the sight of a spectre; his sword fell from his hand; the flush of anger died on his cheek; and he stood for some moments mute and motionless, like an apparition of the drowned.

"The boon," said he, at length recovering his self-possession, "is too worthless for thy asking. I would I had been commanded to fetch thee the head of the king of the Mohammedans, or to do some other service worthy of thy beauty, fair Beatrix, and of my loyalty!"

"Loyalty!" repeated the lady, half in scorn, half in anger. The knight sighed heavily; and after losing some moments in the purgatory of painful remembrance, his thoughts, reverting to the circumstances of his present situation, fixed eagerly upon the object apparently best qualified to afford them ostensible employment.

"How, dog!" he cried, striding up to the still dripping vassal, "hast thou not the grace even to thank the condescension which stoops to care for thy base and worthless life? Down on thy knees, false cur—crouch!" and catching Hugues by the throat, he hurled him to the feet of his patroness.

"Enough, enough," said the lady; "get thee gone, thou naughty fish-seller; St. Gildas be thy speed, and teach thee another time to have more faith in the water, when the need of thy lord requires thee to represent the worthy person of the Sire of Keridreux!" Hugues kissed the hem of the mantle of his fair preserver, and coasting distantly round his master, dived into the crowd and disappeared.

While with the grave pace and solemn countenance of a Breton knight, the Sire of Keridreux strode stately along in the townward direction by the side of the lady, his lank hair and dripping garments seemed to afford considerable amusement to the spectators. The bourgeois concealed their merriment only till he had passed to a distance at which it would be safe to laugh; and the nobles, partly from politeness and partly from prudence, were fain to put their gloves upon their mouths. The knight, however, seemed to have forgotten his late disaster and present plight, in considerations of more moment. He turned his head neither to the right nor to the left, but stalked mutely and majestically along, till on arriving at the house where his fair companion resided, the bubbling sound that attended his plunging into an arm-chair recalled his wandering thoughts.

"The beast!" he muttered," the outcast dog! To serve me such a trick, and in her presence; after I had arrayed myself in all respects befitting the dignity of the spurs, and journeyed hither on purpose to get speech of her! Beatrix," he continued aloud, and seizing hold of her hand with his wet gloves,—"fairest Beatrix, deign to regard with compassion the most miserable of the slaves of thy beauty!"

"Indeed I do," said Beatrix, with grave simplicity,— "the weather begins now to get cold, and these wet clothes must be both unpleasant and dangerous. I think I hear the cry of 'cupping!' in the street;[15] allow me to persuade thee to lose a little blood."

"An ocean in a cause of thine!" replied the Knight, "but by a lance, fair Beatrix, not a lancet; I had ever a horror of losing blood otherwise than in a fair field."

"Then at least a draught of wine will fortify thy bowels against the cold; and here stands a flask of the true Paris brewing, to which our wines of Brittany are mere cider."[16] She then decanted about a modern quart into a huge silver cup, which she presented to the knight.

"Let it receive virtue from thy lip," said the Knight, hesitatingly, "or I shall find none."

"Nay, nay, fair sir," replied Beatrix, "those days are past and gone. We *have* eaten, it is true, out of the

---

[15] The physician, in these days, cried, like Wisdom, in the streets. "Ventouses à ventouser!" was the burthen; cupping being the principal business of the profession. He was generally accompanied by a female partner, whose office it was to assist ladies in their accouchement. The latter would be unnecessary at present, as the French women of the nineteenth century prefer having men to officiate on such occasions.

[16] The wines of the environs of Paris, *mirabile dictu,* were anciently celebrated. Andreas Baccius (1524-1600), in his treatise *De Vineis,* printed at Rome in 1596, says that they do not yield to any in the kingdom; and a century after, Chaulieu represents the Marquis of la Fare as going to Surène and drinking so freely of them, that he could not well find the door:

> "Et l'on m'óeris qu'à Surêne
> Au cabaret, on a vu
> La Fare, et le bon Silène,
> Qui, pour en avoir trop bu,
> Retrouvoient la porte à peine
> D'un lieu qu'ils ont tant connu."

same dish, and drunken out of the same cup, but what was only folly then would be sin and shame now."[17] The Knight raised the goblet gloomily to his mouth.

"I trust," said Beatrix, while she stooped, as if to look for something among the rushes on the floor,— "I trust that the worthy Dame of Keridreux is in good health?" The Knight started at the question, and was seized with a fit of coughing which spoiled his draught.

"Confusion upon the name!" he cried, dashing the remainder of the wine upon the floor. "Would to heaven she were in the health I wish her! And it is thou, cruel as thou art, and fair as thou art cruel, who hast bound me to a stake as doleful as the cross—who hast leagued me, I verily believe, with an incarnate fiend!"

"I have heard," said Beatrix, demurely, but with sparkling eyes, "that the Dame of Keridreux is of somewhat a peculiar temper; but, for my part, I was, as I am, only a simple maiden, and no liege sovereign to give in marriage my vassals at my pleasure."

"Oh, would thou hadst been less my liege sovereign—or more! I loved thee, Beatrix, as a man and a soldier; I knew nothing, not I, of the idle affectation which plays with a true servant even as an angler tickles a trout; I received thy seeming slight as a purposed insult—and straightway went home, and married another in pure fury and despite."

"Alas, alas!" said Beatrix, weeping, "thou wert ever of a fierce and sudden temper! Thou knewest not of the modern fashion of noble and knightly love. Having plighted thy troth, and drunk with me of the

---

[17] To have only one plate and one cup at table was a mark of gallantry and good understanding between a lady and gentleman. In the old romance of "Perceforet," in describing a feast of eight hundred knights, it is said, "Et si n'y oust celuy (personne) qui n'eust une dame ou une pu- celle à son écuelle." Drinking out of the same cup is still a token of love in some parts of Lower Brittany.

cup of faith and unity, thou dreamedst not of aught save holy wedlock after the manner of our ancestors. It entered not into thy brain to imagine that the lays of the minstrel were to be verified in the history of private life, and that thou wert to enter into human happiness, as the soul attains to heaven, through the portals of doubt, fear, sorrow, suffering, yea, even despair. Alack-a-day! Peradventure I was myself to blame; peradventure I disguised the too great softness of my heart by too stony a hardness of the face, and looked to thee, alas! for more patience and forbearance in the conduct than there was constancy in the soul. But God's will be done!" continued she, drying her eyes. "Time and Our Lady's benevolence will straighten all things, even the crooked temper—if crooked it be—of the Dame of Keridreux."

"Serpent!" exclaimed the knight, bitterly, "thou knowest not what she is. Oh, if I could find but one leper spot on her body for twenty on her soul!"

"Hush! hush!" interrupted the lady, hastily, thou forgettest that although the laws of man are silent, those of God still speak with a voice of thunder to the transgressor!"[18]

"But thou knowest her not," repeated the knight. "Oh, I could tell thee what would turn thy young blood cold but to hear!"

"Then tell me," said Beatrix, "for I love to have my blood run cold."

"Alas, alas!" ejaculated the sorrowful husband, "she understands Latin!"[19]

---

[18] The new and terrible disease of leprosy was held to form a proper lesson for divorce, although this was not sanctioned by any express law.

[19] Women who understood Latin were held in especial horror by the Bretons; and many stories such as that which follows were told to account for or excuse the feeling. Female learning has in all ages been hated by male ignorance. The classification in the following stanza is odd:

"La femme qui parle Latin,

"Latin! Holy Virgin, bow I pity thee! Out on the false heart! it could not be without a price she bought that knowledge. It was but last Easter that one of those learned dames in the neighbourhood of the convent where I board, sat upon a viper's eggs, and produced a winged serpent with three heads, whose nourishment to this hour, as all men relate, is human blood." The gallant knight grew pale at this anecdote; but after swallowing down another goblet-full of wine at a draught, he hemmed stoutly, and again seizing the hand of his sometime love—

"Beatrix," said he, suddenly, "I am weary of my life; I have come to the determination of abandoning my inheritance, and passing over into Italy. Fly with me! I will either beg or buy a dispensation from the pope, and make thee my wife in Rome." Beatrix opened her eyes in astonishment, mingled with horror. Turning away her head in aversion, she looked towards the window. The shades of evening were beginning to fall, and at the moment the distant howl of a wolf in the neighbouring forest struck upon her ear. The maiden shuddered at the ominous sound. Spitting in sign of abhorrence,[20] while she crossed herself devoutly—

"Alas!" she exclaimed,—"unhappy wretch! knowest thou not that in Italy—ay, even in Spain, or England, thou wouldst still be under the jurisdiction of the laws of Heaven? Are we not assured that such transgressor shuts upon himself the gates of Paradise—and with a wife like thine, couldst thou expect them to re-open? Would the vixen Dame of Keridreux, beseeching the permission of Saint Peter, come to thee at thy cry, and exclaim through the

---

L'enfant qui est nourri de vin,
Soleil qui luiserne au matin,
Ne vient point à bonne fin."
PIERRE GROSNET (1460-1540)

[20] The usual token of the times.

bars, 'I forgive thee!'"[21] The knight groaned, and applied again to the wine-goblet.

"Art thou not afraid," resumed the lady, "to go home to thy lonely abode, and at so late an hour, with a mortal sin in thy thoughts? Perchance the howl of that prowling wolf was an omen sent by Our Lady herself to warn thee; and now, while I recall it— holy saints—methought the voice sounded like thine own!"

"Saint Yves, and Saint Brieuc!" cried the knight, starting suddenly upon his legs—"thou dost not mean it! No longer ago than last night I dreamed that I was myself transformed into a loup-garou; and at Easter the misbegotten cur who dragged me to-day into the river, saw with his own eyes the Leader of Wolves coming out of the very pool where I plunged!"[22]

Beatrix changed colour at this intelligence, and as the room became darker and darker, began to wish her unhallowed lover away.

"Repent," said she—"repent while there is yet time; I will myself beseech Our Lady du Roncier in thy behalf. Good-night, good-night—and Heaven hold thee from turning a loup-garou!" The knight, true to the Breton custom, having first ascertained that there was no more wine in the jar,[23] made his obeisance with a heavy sigh, and left the house without uttering another word.

---

[21] The formula of admission for naughty husbands.—"Les Evangiles des Connoilles," Jean Mareschal, p. 101, 1493.

[22] The superstition of the loup-garou held the sinners of Brittany in awe for a considerable time. The guilty found themselves transformed into wolves for a space short or long, in proportion to the magnitude of the offence; but it is said that in process of years, men became so audacious, that some individuals sought, from an odd and vicious taste, the metamorphoses which their fathers had endured as punishment. The Leader mentioned was an apparition of a grim, lank personage, followed by a string of spectre wolves.

[23] The Low Bretons, in their quality, no doubt, of descendants of the Celts, are said to have been a grave, melancholy race, much addicted to drinking, fanciful, and superstitious.

His conversation with Beatrix having been greatly fuller than it has been thought necessary to report, it was now late in the evening, being past eight o'clock. The streets were deserted, and the houses shut up; and most of the inhabitants, having supped two hours ago, were beginning to think of retiring to bed.[24] On emerging from the dark and lonely street, where the rows of tall houses inclined their heads to each other in gossip fashion, the knight, with unsteady step, and head bewildered both by love and wine, took the way to the bridge. While walking cautiously over the creaking planks, a hum of distant voices rose upon his ear, and presently a small solitary light appeared dancing wildly upon the troubled waters. He stood still in awe and curiosity, till at length the light was suddenly extinguished, and the voice ceased; and muttering a prayer for the drowned, whose corpse was thus sought for, and miraculously pointed out, he resumed his journey.[25]

The shades of evening fell more thickly around every moment, and the sire began to regret his bootless journey, and to look sharply about at the solitary tree or tall stone which stood here and there with an unpleasant perpendicularity near the road-side. In those days, trees and stones were not the only objects of curiosity which presented themselves to the gaze of the night traveller. Men, housed in their towers, and castles, and cottages, were accustomed piously to leave the kingdom of literal darkness to those whom it more concerned; and when accident compelled some luckless wayfarer to encroach upon forbidden hours, he looked upon himself as an intruder where he had no business,

---

[24] "Lever à six, diner à dix,
Souper à six, coucher à dix,
Fait vivre l'homme dix fois dix."
                              Old Proverb.

[25] When the body of a drowned person could not readily be found, a candle was stuck into a loaf and sent adrift upon the water. The light, of course, put itself out at the proper spot.

and where he was exceedingly likely to meet with the chastisement he deserved. Like most persons in a similar situation, the knight experienced a marvellous increase in piety as he went along. He repeated an *Ave* at every step; and on arriving at the different confluences of little village paths, where crosses were raised to serve AS direction-posts to the dead who might be disposed to revisit their relations,[26] he stood still, and prayed aloud, with perfect sincerity, for the repose of their souls.

Further on, having reached a stream which, leaping out of a wood, crossed the road, he paused in doubt as to the depth,—for, in truth, his brain was somewhat confused with the wine he had drunk. On raising his head he was startled to see a lady standing among the trees at the water's edge. She was dressed in white, and, as well as he could distinguish, very elegantly formed; but her face was concealed from him, as she bent over the stream busily engaged in wringing a garment which she had apparently just washed. An unpleasant sensation swept across the mind of the Sire of Keridreux; and although a man of distinguished courage, and devotedly attached to the fair sex (for all his wife belonged to it), he plunged suddenly knee-deep into the water, and made for the opposite bank.

Attracted by the sound, the lady raised her head.

"Sir Knight," she exclaimed, in a voice of touching sweetness—"tarry, I pray thee, for the love of honour, and help me to wring this garment, which is all too heavy for my slender fingers!" The knight, half alarmed and half ashamed, turned back, and leaping into the wood, seized hold of the dripping garment which she presented to him. He twisted to the right; but the lady was twisting the same way.

"We are wrong," said she, with good-humour. The knight tried again, but with the same effect—again—

---

[26] Louise-Adolphe Thiers, Traité de Superst. t. 1, p. 71.

and again; and as at last he perceived with whom he had to deal, his hair bristled upon his head, and cold drops of sweat trickled down his brow. But still he continued the bootless labour, twisting, straining, praying, and perspiring, till at length the garment fell into the water, and danced away like a bubble on the stream; and the false washerwoman, breaking into shrieks of wild laughter, disappeared among the trees.[27]

The knight made but one leap across the river, and regaining the firm road, recommenced his journey with as much speed as could well be exerted by legs which would not be said to run. His brain, unsettled before, was turned completely topsy-turvy by this adventure; the air was thick with shadows; his ears were filled with strange voices; and at length, as the substantial howl of a wolf arose from the neighbouring thicket, it was echoed by a cry as wild and dismal from his own lips. His dream of the loup-garou—the warning of Beatrix—the horrible similarity she had detected in the voices of the wolf and the man—all rushed upon his heart like a deluge.

At the instant, a sound resembling a human cry floated upon the sluggish wind: it approached nearer and nearer, seeming one moment a shout of menace, the next a call for aid, and the next a moan of agony. Sometimes it appeared to melt away in the distance, and sometimes the heart of the traveller died within him as it crept close to his very heels. In vain he tugged with unstrung fingers at his sword—in vain he essayed to produce one pious ejaculation from his

---

[27] This lady was no doubt one of that unearthly sisterhood known to the Bretons by the name of the "Laveuses de Nuit." Had the Knight refused to wring with her, he would have fared much worse; and if he had only thought of looking about the spot when the task was ended, it is not improbable that he would have found the drops which fell from the garment metamorphosed into pearls and other precious stones.

dry lips; and at length, fairly subdued by the horrors of his situation, he betook himself to open flight.

The voice of the Crieuses de Nuit pursued him,[28]—his brain began to wander. His rapid steps sounded to his ears like the galloping of a four-footed animal; he rubbed his sleeve upon his face, and was convinced for the moment that he wore a coat of fur, forgetting that his own beard produced the peculiarity of friction: but at length, somewhat relieved by the rattling of his sword, and the jingling of his spurs, he thanked Our Lady du Roncier that he was still no loup-garou.

The night in the mean time was getting darker and darker; the road, where it crossed a plain, became less distinguishable from the bare and level soil at the sides; and at length the traveller, deviating by little and little, lost the track altogether. Still, however, he continued to run on,—for in mortal fear one cares not about the whither, contented with escape, even if it should be to a worse danger. And so it happened with the Sire of Keridreux; for in flying from what, after all, was but perhaps a mere sound—*vox et præterea nihil*[29]—he stumbled upon a substantial misadventure.

On diving down a sudden declivity, with even more velocity than he had calculated on, he found himself all at once in the midst of at least a dozen men, dressed from head to foot in white robes. The abrupt visiter paused in astonishment and dismay, as a shout of welcome rang in his ears,

"Hail, Sire of Keridreux!" cried one.

"Hail, husband of the dame who understands Latin!" another.

"Hail, guilty lover of Beatrix!" a third.

"Hail, magnanimous ducker in the fisherman's well!" a fourth; and so on, till the whole had spoken; each speaker, when he had finished, whirling swiftly

---

[28] Cousins of the Laveuses de Nuit.

[29] A voice and nothing more

round on one foot like a vaulter at a merry-meeting. When every man had thus given his welcome, the strange group continued their revolutions in silence for some minutes, their white garments floating round them like vapour agitated by the wind. They at length stopped suddenly, and shouted with one voice, "Hail LOUP-GAROU!" and presently there began so surprising a din of baying and howling, that a whole forest of wolves could not have produced the like.

The knight listened at first in terror, but by degrees he began to howl himself as if in emulation. The louder he howled, however, the louder rose the voices of his companions; and he threw away his head gear, and spread back his beard to give his voice play. Thus, by degrees, he tore off his clothes, piece by piece, till at last he found himself howling *in cuerpo.*[30] His comrades then caught him by the hand, and joining hands also with one another, they formed a ring, and began to dance round a great stone standing on end in the midst. Round and round danced the trees, and the rocks, and the hills, and the whole world, in the eyes of the knight; and to his stunned ears every stone had a voice, every leaf and clod its individual howl. Round flew the dancers—faster, and faster, and faster; till the Sire of Keridreux sank gasping upon the ground, and the White Men, springing into the air with a " whirr!" disappeared from his sight.[31]

When his recollection returned, he found himself lying upon the same spot, stark naked. It was now daylight, and he heard the sunrise horn sounding from a watch-tower in the neighbourhood. Gathering himself up, stiff, bruised, and exhausted, he looked round, and discovered with no small satisfaction that he stood upon his own ground. The castle of

[30] In the nude

[31] These gentry were the Hommes Blancs, of the same family as the Laveuses and Crieuses de Nuit.

Keridreux was close at hand, and the scene of his adventure was the corner of a belt of wood which on one side protected the fortress. Having collected his scattered garments, he dressed as well as he could, and went straight home.

The Dame of Keridreux was in bed when her lord arrived, and as he entered the apartment, she raised herself on her elbow, and prepared, with eyes glowing like two live coals, to discharge upon his devoted head the wrath she had been nursing for him the whole night. There was something, however, peculiar in his appearance this morning. In his jaded and haggard air she could discern few of the accusing witnesses of debauchery she had so often produced against him; and his scared look, she saw at a glance, was wholly unconnected with conjugal awe. The lady, therefore, suffered her husband to undress without a single remark, and to throw himself into bed at an hour when more sprightly spouses were sallying forth to the chase.

Altering her usual plan of operations, she crept close to where be lay, and throwing her arm round him, heaved a deep sigh. The knight sprang with a suppressed oath from her embrace, and took refuge in a more distant part of the bed; a thing which it was not difficult to do at a period when such articles of household furniture were usually twelve feet long, and of a proportionate breadth.[32]

"Alas!" sighed the lady, in a tender tone, "how dreary are the hours of night that are passed in the absence of a beloved husband!" The knight groaned.

"Where hast thou been, thou runaway?" continued she—"where hast thou been, my baron?"[33]

"I have been," said the knight—"Oh!" and he groaned again.

---

[32] In the cottages the whole family slept in the same bed; and this, it would seem, from the enormous size of the beds, must at one time have been the custom even among the higher classes.

[33] A common title given by ladies to their lords.—"Le Grand d'Aussi Vie des Anciens," t. 1, p. 339.

"Alack-a-day!" sighed the dame, once more—"I slept not a wink the live-long night. I feared that some mischance had befallen thee; and the wolves in the forest kept such a howling—"

"It was I who howled!" said the knight, suddenly.

"Thou! nay, now thou art mocking me; the merry wine still dances in thy brain—thou who howled?"

"By the holy Virgin!" said the knight, "it was none other than my comrades and I!"

"Thou art mad to say it; thou art deeper in the wine-cups than I thought. Where hast thou been?" continued she, sharply—"where wert thou all night?"

"I was dancing in the wood," said the knight, sleepily and sulkily—"and I howled,"—yawning.

"*Why* didst thou howl?" inquired the lady, with fierce curiosity.

"I howled because I was a wolf, and could not choose!"

"O ho!" said she, as the knight dropped asleep—"O ho!" Then stirring him gently, and placing her lips to his ear—

"What part of the wood," she whispered, "my own baron?"

"At the corner," replied the half-unconscious knight, "where stands the great stone—cursed be its gener-a-ti-on!" and he slept aloud.

The day was far advanced before the Sire of Keridreux awoke. He found, as usual, at his bedside his vassal Hugues; who indeed, besides his numerous other capacities, was a sort of body squire, or feudal valet (in the modern sense of the word), and superintended more particularly the dress and toilet of his master. Hugues on this occasion had much of the air of one of the class of quadrupeds we have mentioned, when his tail, technically speaking, is between his legs: he stood edgewise to his master, with his face in such a position as to give him the advantage of eying with equal perspicuousness the lord on the one hand and the open door on the other, while his feet were so planted upon the rushes that at a word or a look he could have vanished, in the manner vulgarly called "a bolt."

The knight, however, seemed to have been sweated out of his Celtic irascibility; for, although conscious that to the villainous trick of his dependant he owed all his misfortunes, he turned upon him a look more in sorrow than in anger.

"Alas!" said he, with a heavy sigh, "that he who has eaten of my bread, and drunk of my cup, with all his uncles and grandmothers before him, should at last have served me so unrighteous a turn!"

"I could not help it," replied Hugues, whimpering, yet deriving courage from the placid grief of his master—"St. Gildas is my judge, I could not help it! Yet what, my master! it was but a ducking at the best; only fancy it rain water, and it will be dry before thou hast time to take off thy morning's draught."

"Out on thee, false knave!" said the knight— "thinkest thou I care for a wet doublet? It was not the water, alas! but the wine—"

"Holy saints! and what have I to do with that?" ejaculated Hugues. "If it was not water—ay, and right foul and muddy water too—that thou and I played our gambols in, may I never taste another drop of wine in my life!"

"It was the wine, Hugues—and yet it was the water; for thou shalt know that a superabundance of the one can only be cured by a like quantity of the other. And yet, alas! it was not the wine, but the lateness of the hour; although this being the consequence of the lapse of time, and that of the action of drinking, which again was caused by water, thou, beast that thou art! art at the bottom of all.— Well, well, what is passed and gone may not now be helped; it behooves a wise man to enjoy the present and prepare for the future: hand me therefore my morning's draught, and let us consider of what is to be done; for I vow and protest that I do perspire from my very inmost marrow at the thoughts of the approaching night!" The sire then raising himself up in bed, with the assistance of Hugues, applied to his lips, at short intervals, a capacious silver flagon filled with hippocras, and between whiles narrated at full length to the confidant the story of his mishaps.

In the consultation which followed it was determined that Hugues should start off incontinent on a fleet steed with a letter to Father Etienne of Ploërmel, the knight's confessor, imploring his immediate presence at the castle of Keridreux; and it was fondly hoped that, by virtue of the prayers and anathemas of that holy man, the evil hour of twilight, when the sire might otherwise expect to be driven forth to resume the nightly character of a loup-garou, would pass over in peace.

"Hie thee away, good Hugues—hie thee away!" said the knight; "ride for life and death, if thou lovest me; and as the holy monk is somewhat of the slowest in equestrian matters, even fix a pillion to thy own horse, and fetch him hither behind thee."

It was not the custom of the Dame of Keridreux to permit egress from the castle without knowing all the whys and wherefores of the matter; and Hugues, who had been trained to turn and double like a hare in such cases, hesitated as to the plan he should adopt to smuggle himself out. Recollecting, however, that in whatever manner he might manage for himself, it would be difficult to compel his steed to crawl upon knees and haunches, or even to repress the joyful neigh with which he was wont to enter upon a journey—and moreover, bethinking himself that, in reality, there was nothing detrimental to the power and dignity of the dame in her husband's desiring to see his confessor in circumstances so critical, he went boldly to the stable, and saddled his horse, only taking care to conceal the pillion with an old cloak, for fear of raising the devil in the jealous mind of his mistress.

"And whither away, good Hugues?" asked the lady, popping in her head just at the moment when man

and horse were about to dart from the stable—
"whither away so fast, and whither away so late?"

"To Ploërmel," answered Hugues, "with the permission of God."

"And thine errand, if it be not a secret?"

"To order a mass to be said for the deliverance of my master from the power of evil spirits."

"A right holy errand! Our Lady speed thee, amen!"

"Amen!" repeated Hugues; and scarcely conscious that he had told a lie, so much was he in the habit of that figure of speech when in conversation with the dame, he was in the act of clapping his heels to his horse's sides.

"Stay!" said the lady; "I bethink me that I have here a memorandum for my own confessor at Ploërmel; and truly it is the duty of a good wife to seek assistance from holy church, in circumstances so strange and trying. Deliver this with commendations to Father Bonaventure; thou wilt distinguish it from thy master's, if he have given a written order for the mass, by its want both of seal and address; for the thoughts of the innocent require no protection from the curiosity either of men or spirits."

When Hugues, who loved a good gallop with all his heart, arrived at the oak of Mi-voie, he bethought himself of his despatches, and slackening his pace, pulled them forth from his breast, to assure Himself of their safety.

"This is my lady's," thought he; "for although I cannot read a single letter, yet I have learning enough to know that here there is neither seal nor address; while the other—Holy Mary! what hath come to pass?" and turning it round in consternation, he discovered that the second letter was in precisely the same predicament. The knight, in his anxiety and confusion had forgotten the customary forms; arid the two letters, to the unpractised eyes of Hugues, were as indistinguishable as two peas. Although sorely afraid, however of the consequences of a blunder, where the vixen dame of Keridreux was concerned, he determined stoutly to be in the right on his master's side, and to try Father Etienne with both, should the first prove to be the wrong one. Fortifying himself with this resolution, he resumed his gallop, and speedily came within sight of the town of Ploërmel.

The avenues to this town were nothing more than the tracks from the neighbouring huts and castles; no great road appeared in its vicinity, like an artery, spreading wealth abroad into its dependencies; and no navigable river or canal supplied the want of a highway on terra firma. For this reason Ploërmel, although a considerable place, had something singularly melancholy and solitary in its aspect; the houses too were old and black; and the convent, now visible on the brow of a hill, seemed to guard with sullen austerity the strange quiet of the scene.[34] Hugues crossed himself mechanically as he entered the town, and mentally resolved that nothing short of sorcery should detain him beyond sunset within its precincts.

Father Etienne was a precise and somewhat sour-looking elderly man, and Hugues was rejoiced to find, on delivery of the letter, that he had committed no mistake. The priest's countenance expressed both the grief and surprise that were natural on such an occasion; and after a moment's deliberation he told the messenger that he should be ready to accompany him to Keridreux in a few minutes. He then retired to read over again without witnesses the singular epistle he had received, which ran as follows:—

"I fear thy ingratitude for my preference; yet nevertheless, I would confer with thee in private this

---

[34] Two centuries later, a magnificent convent of Carmelites was founded on the same site by John II. (1239-1305) Count of Richemond. The cloister was composed of seventy-two vaults, and in the middle there was a well of limpid water, surmounted by a beautiful dove-cote. This edifice was destroyed in the wars of the League.

evening on matters which may concern us both. My husband, it seems, is translated into a loup-garou! I would inquire whether there be not force enough in thy prayers to restore him to his human form, and deprive him of the power of getting into mischief again. If thou understand me not, stay where thou art; but if thou be what I take thee for, and would fain find thee, come to me in the dusk, ascend the private stair, for fear of interruption, and I will meet thee in the closet."

"Oh, woman, woman!" exclaimed the priest; "and will nothing less than a monk content thee? and a monk of my standing in the convent, and of my sanctity of character? But, nevertheless, I will go— yea, I will attend the rendezvous, and inquire into the real situation of my poor son in the spirit, the Knight of Keridreux. Peradventure the dame will not offer violence; but if she does, I will struggle in prayer and invocation,—no saint will I leave unsummoned, and no martyred virgin unsolicited. But, in the mean time, it is necessary to beware of Brother Bonaventure, the dame's former confessor, whose eyes, as sharp at all times as those of a lynx, will now be made ten times more so by jealousy and wounded vanity. Let me first see that the coast is clear, and then steal out to— what may betide."

Father Bonaventure, to whom Hugues delivered the other letter, was a sleek, plump, oily monk of thirty-five, with an appearance of great good-humour in his countenance, belied at second sight by a sinister cast in one eye.

"Hum!" said he, reading the epistle of the afflicted knight; "this is well; the influence of the dame must have gone far indeed, when the Sire of Keridreux sends to *me* for a shrift or a benison! But can there be no blunder?—Hark thee, fellow, from whom hadst thou this letter?"

"From the Dame of Keridreux."

"Right, right; why, this is as it should be; but as for the loup-garou, and the midnight howling,—Hark thee again, fellow,—how didst thou leave thy master?"

"Queerish, may it please your holiness—a little queerish."

"Drunk—I thought so. I'faith, she is a clever woman, that Dame of Keridreux. To make her very husband send for me! But we must have a care of brother Etienne, the knight's confessor; the rogue half suspects me already; and when he knows that I have supplanted him with the husband, there will be no keeping his jealous eyes from my affair with the wife. In the mean time, let us see that the coast is clear, and then hie we to inquire into the malady of our loup-garou."

Hugues, being at length dismissed by Father Bonaventure, ran anxiously to Father Etienne, to entreat him to mount and away; but the latter encountering his brother monk on his road to the stable-door, where the horse waited, pretended to have forgotten something, and hastily re-entered the convent. As for Father Bonaventure, he started back with the same confusion, and from the same cause, so that neither perceived the perplexity of the other; and thus the two rivals kept playing at bo-peep till Hugues was ready to tear his beard for very vexation. The sun at length set, and the warder's horn sounding from tower to tower, struck upon the heart of the faithful squire like a voice of despair.

"A curse on that monk," cried he, "and on all his grandfathers! Does he mean to transport the relics of the convent, one by one, to our castle, that he thus goes and comes, and fetches and carries, without beginning or end? My poor master will he out in the forest, and stripped to the buff, long before we reach Keridreux; and at every howl we hear on that lonely road, I am sure my heart will leap higher in my mouth than it did when I plunged head foremost into the fisherman's well."

Father Etienne, at this moment, approached to within a single pace of the expectant horse; and while he stopped to look cautiously about him, Hugues, at the last grain of patience, and in the fear of his life that the monk meant to turn tail again, whipped him up in his arms, and clapping him upon the saddle, sprang himself upon the pillion behind, and made off with his prize at full gallop. The terrified ecclesiastic, seizing fast hold of the horse's mane with one hand, and of Hugues's uncombed beard with the other, kept his seat with admirable firmness, the motion of the animal jolting out sometimes a prayer and sometimes a curse, as they happened to come uppermost; while the venturous squire, looking pertinaciously to the quarter of their destination, already beginning to be covered with the shades of evening, and laying it stoutly into the horse with whip, spur, and tongue, all at one moment, had no time to think of the sacrilege he committed in stealing a churchman.

In the mean time, Father Bonaventure perceiving the absence of his rival, although without imagining the cause, led his own palfrey in an instant out of the stable, and leaping nimbly on his back, scoured off in the same direction. The first monk no sooner observed the pursuit, than in the confused consciousness of intended secrecy, and perhaps of not overly virtuous intention, he uttered a cry of alarm, and forgetting his dread of equestrian exercises, began to belabour the beast with his heels, and shower upon him the verbal insults which all over the world have so powerful an effect on the exertions of the sensitive and intelligent horse. Hugues, terrified at this exhibition of terror, did not dare to look round for the cause, but griped the monk still closer in his arms, and whipped, and spurred, and prayed with all his might; while Father Bonaventure, seeing a double-loaded steed maintain the *pas* so bravely, began to fear that his own nag was only trifling with him, and putting heel, and whip, and voice into furious requisition, dashed helter-skelter, neck or nothing, after.

On went the horsemen as if a whole legion of devils were at their heels; and it would have been an even bet which should gain the race, had not Father Bonaventure's palfrey suddenly stumbled in leaping a ditch. When Father Etienne saw his pursuer disappear all at once from the face of the earth, he was struck dumb with amazement; but soon, attributing the appearance to what seemed its probable cause, he wiped the sweat from his brow, and anathematized the phantom horseman with the bitterest curses of the church.

In a few minutes more he was set down at his destination; and Hugues, without even waiting to receive a blessing for his safe conduct, dragged his horse abruptly and sulkily to the stable, swearing to himself, by every saint he could remember, that he would never ride double with a priest again in his life.

Although it was only dusk out of doors, when Father Etienne gained the secret stair he found himself in utter darkness. He had not groped his way long, however, till he heard a "hist!" sounding along the corridor; and presently the Dame of Keridreux, encountering his hand, very unceremoniously threw her arm round his neck.

"And at last, my ghostly father!" said she, in a whisper, "what in the name of all the devils has detained thee? Another moment would have ruined all; for out of very madness, I would either have sworn a conspiracy against thee to the knight, or poniard myself, where I stood here, by turns shivering and burning, in this cold, dark corridor."

Father Etienne blessed himself secretly that he was as yet only on the threshold of an intrigue with such a firebrand; and feeling his heart beat strongly, nay almost audibly, with virtuous resolution, he began to cast about for some means of edging himself out of the adventure.

"Thou knowest," continued the dame, with a sort of chuckle which made her confidant's blood run cold, "that the only way to deprive a loup-garou of the faculty of resuming his human shape in the morning, is to take away the clothes which he strips off on his conversion into a wolf.[35] Ha! ha! I cannot choose but laugh to think of my dear baron coming smelling, and smelling in vain, for his doublet. How he would glare and snort—ha! ha!—and howl—hoo-oo-oo! Father Etienne's hair stood on end as the malicious dame, with impressible gayety, began to howl in imitation of a wolf; nor was his horror lessened when, shortly after, a sound resembling an echo appeared to come from the direction of the knight's chamber.

"As I live," cried the lady, "he is at it already! Now will he forth presently into the wood to turn a loup-garou; and what we have to do must be done at once. Stay where thou art; stir not; speak not for thy life, till I come again!" and the dame glided along the corridor towards the chamber of her lord.

Father Etienne was no sooner left alone than, throwing himself upon his hands and knees, for fear of doing himself a mischief upon the steep dark stairs, he crept down like a cat, and with stealthy pace betook himself to the stable, determined to saddle the first horse he could lay hands upon, and ride full speed home to his convent, were it at the

---

[35] Tristan le Voyageur. This agreeable traveler tells a story of a certain lord translated into a loup-garou, whose wife's gallant steals his clothes. The unhappy wolf wanders for many days through the forest, till accidentally meeting the duke when hunting, he forgets his present plight, makes a very gentlemanly obeisance, and falls into the line of courtiers. He is carried to the palace as a prodigy, caressing and caressed by all; till seeing his base supplanter enter the room, he suddenly springs at his throat, and is with difficulty prevented from tearing him to pieces. Whereupon the wife and the gallant are arrested, confess their misdeeds, and restore the clothes; and the loup-garou becomes a man again. The motto alludes to this story. As for the apparently trifling circumstance of dress making all the difference between a wolf and a lord of those times, thereby hangs a *tail* or a sequence, which might be twisted into a pretty moral.

hazard of a hundred necks. It was now, however, quite dark; and although he could hear the panting of a steed, there was either no saddle in the stable, or it was hung out of his reach. In this predicament he lay down upon the straw, and waited in great agitation for the coming of some of the servants.

A considerable time elapsed, and the meditations of the holy man became more confused every moment; till at length Hugues, bearing in one hand a lantern, and with the other dragging a large bundle, made his appearance at the stable-door. "Oh heavens!" said he, holding up his lantern, "and is it thou after all? Well, I thought my lady must have been wrong when she talked of a monk and his palfrey, for here be no monks but thou, and no palfreys but my own precious Dapple."

"I pray thee, son," said the father, "tell me no more of thy lady, but take me incontinent to the place thou broughtest me from, if thou settest aught of value on the prayers of a wretched but holy monk."

"Well, did ever mortal hear the like! I take thee, quotha! May the great dev— No matter. At an hour like this, and my master just turning a loup-garou, and after thou thyself, monk though thou be, didst nothing but screech and sweat with fear all the way hither, although the darkness was no more to be compared to this than heaven is to hell! I take thee! I will see thee nay, I say nothing; there is my precious Dapple, whom I love *as* my own soul,—take *him*, he is thine for this night. Mount, mount, and be thankful, since thou wilt travel at such untimely hours; and if thou dost not pray heartily for the lender, monk though thou be, thou wilt surely go to—Ploërmel by some worse conveyance! There, thou sittest like a knight—On with thee, in the name of Saint Gildas!"

The monk having suffered Hugues, without expostulation, to perch him upon the horse, and fasten the bundle, although wherefore, he was too down-hearted to take the trouble of asking, behind him, set forth upon his dreary road with no other sign of farewell than a heavy sigh.

While wayfaring gently along, with the perfect concurrence of Dapple, on whose spirits the late race had had a sedative effect, his thoughts were busy with the circumstances of this strange journey. It was evident that some traitorous design was on foot against the knight. Who were the conspirators? Why, the Dame of Keridreux, and he himself, Father Etienne! His presence at the castle on the fatal night, if fatal it was to be, could be proved; he had met the lady by special appointment in secrecy and darkness, and she had imparted her evil intentions without a word of disapprobation on his part. Thus it appeared that his own safety was inextricably wound up with that of the lady; and the monk cursed from the bottom of his bowels the unlucky stars which had made him a party perhaps to a murder, or at least to the impiety of condemning an unfortunate gentleman to the forest for life, in the capacity of a wolf.

He arrived at the convent without further adventure; but, when unsaddling the horse, was surprised to observe the bundle, which, in the confusion of his mind, he had taken for a pillion.[36] He carried it notwithstanding to his cell, telling the porter, in reply to his questions, that it contained a cloak and other habits he had received as a gift. Unfortunate falsehood—as true as any truth he could have told! It was in reality the cloak and other every-day habits of the Knight of Keridreux! The monk, thunderstruck at this new calamity, gazed upon the articles in silence. He felt all the horrors of actual guilt, and all the contrition of sincere repentance; he looked upon himself as a convicted criminal in the eyes of God and man, and upon the

---

[36] A spare seat mounted behind the rider of a horse

hose and doublet before him as the true *corpus delicti*[37] of his villany.

"Cursed be the minute in which I was born," cried he, "and the year and the day thereof! Cursed be the steed that bore me on its back on that nefarious errand! And may its master who seized me, even as a prisoner, in the snares of hell never see salvation! What misery is this that has come upon me? Cannot people sin without my sanction? If they imagine treason, am I to be drawn into holes and corners to hatch it! If they murder, can nobody else be found to sharpen the dagger? And if they turn their husbands into beasts, is it still I who must hide the old doublet? Begone, evidences of guilt, and snares of perdition! I spurn ye, filthy rags of unrighteousness! yea, I spurn ye with my foot—" and in a phrensy of rage and fear, he kicked the old clothes about the room, buffeting his breast, and tearing handfuls of hair from his beard.

The next morning he saw Father Bonaventure at matins as usual, looking as if nothing had happened; and his choler re-awoke, as he considered that all the misfortunes of the previous night ought to have fallen by right to him.

"Plague on the wavering fancies of women!" thought he; —"of all the days in the year, what made her send for me at that identical time? And I—I would supplant thee! Ah, rogue, I supplanted thee in good season, if thou but knewest it. From the gallop, and the embrace, down to the old doublet, all should else have been thine—all—all—with a murrain[38] to thee!"

But when the reports, as yet vague and mysterious, at length reached the convent of the misfortune which had befallen the Sire of Keridreux, the unhappy monk was ready to go wild with apprehension. In a few hours more, it was known

---

[37] Evidence of a crime

[38] Highly infectious disease of livestock; literally death

that the knight, for his sins, had been converted into a loup-garou, and that the anxious search instituted by the distracted wife—if we should not rather say widow—had hitherto been productive of no clue either to the man, or to what were of as much importance in such cases, his clothes.

"I will not stand this!" cried Father Etienne, leaping from the bed where he had thrown himself in a fever—"I will not carry off, in a single evening's confessorship, what Brother Bonaventure so richly deserves by the labours of a whole year! By the Holy Virgin, he shall have the old clothes, if I die for it!" and in pursuance of this resolution, the very same evening, he conveyed secretly into his friend's cell the mysterious bundle.

When Father Bonaventure discovered the present, he had not the remotest idea of the real quarter from whence it had come. The dame, on finding her priest absent from the spot where she had directed him to wait, being too far advanced in the business to recede, had sent the bundle by Hugues, merely commanding him to "fix it on the monk's palfrey;" and meeting Father Bonaventure soon after ascending the stairs, the two proceeded to the execution of their plan without explanation, and without being the least aware that a second monk was in the house. On the present occasion, Father Bonaventure, without thinking of any intermediate channel, set down the gift at once as coming from the lady direct; whose fears lie imagined, when the reports and surmises began to buzz, had impelled her thus to get rid of the proofs of their mutual guilt.

"Nay, nay," said he; "I will not put up with this. She might have burned them, if she had chosen; she who has opportunity for such things, and there would have been an end. But to send them to me! Why, what can a monk do with the old clothes of a knight? By my faith, I will not be put upon by any dame of them all! She has as good a right to any risk that is going as I; and they shall e'en find their way back as they came, and let her do with them as she lists."

Hugues, who ever since daybreak had ridden from convent to convent, like one distracted, alarming the enemies of the devil with news of his triumph, and entreating their spiritual aid, arrived at this moment at the religious house of Ploërmel, and presented a fair opportunity to Father Bonaventure to get rid of his bundle. The dependant was easily persuaded to take charge of the precious deposite, which our priest desired him to deliver into the hands of the Dame of Keridreux; and being assured that the ghostly efforts of the monks should be devoted to the cause of his master, he turned his horse's head towards the castle, and began to jog homewards in a melancholy and meditative trot.

He had not journeyed far, ruminating sadly on the transactions of the last two days, when his eye was caught by a projecting corner of the bundle, which was strapped to the rear of his horse. He had not before bestowed much attention on the charge thus committed to his care, nor indeed on the instructions of the monk regarding it; but at this moment some dim associations were suggested to his mind which gradually led his thoughts to the bundle he had fixed on the same place the night before by command of his mistress. The more he gazed, the more his suspicions of its identity were confirmed, and at last, unable to resist the suggestions of that devil (or angel, as it happens) curiosity, he undid the fastenings, and drawing the huge pillion to the front, opened it out. His emotions on discovering the lost suit of his master may be conceived. At first he merely tied it up again, and applying whip and spur with all his might, set forth at headlong speed towards the castle; but in a few moments, as some sudden thought occurred to him, he pulled in the reins with a jerk, which sent the animal back on his haunches.

"Fair and softly!" said he. "Whither, and for what reason, do I haste? If a lady sends a bundle to a monk, and the monk returns the bundle to the lady, it is clear there is some collusion between them. And further, if that bundle be of the clothes of a loup-garou, is it not evident that nothing honest can be meant? Fair and softly, I say again, honest Hugues, and let us consider, as we go along, what is best to be done."

The result of this consideration was a string of resolutions highly favourable to Father Bonaventure, but in nowise redounding to the credit either of the Dame of Keridreux or Father Etienne; and in conclusion, Hugues determined to steal quietly round the castle at nightfall, and, in spite of ghosts and men, to betake himself to the corner of the belt of the forest described by his master, and wait there till the dawn with the clothes, let who would come to claim them.

When it was sufficiently dark for his purpose, he advanced towards the castle, and muffling his horse's heels with handfuls of hay, reached the stable unobserved; then shouldering the bundle, he set out with a good heart for the forest.

While passing an angle of the building, however, a sound met his ear which made him pause. It was of so peculiar a nature, that he was uncertain for the moment whether it came from above, or below, or around, and he therefore stood stock still where he was, in the shadow of the wall. Presently the sound waxed louder, and the ground beside him seemed to tremble and give way; and in another moment a part of what appeared to be a subterranean arch fell in, and disclosed an object from which he recoiled in terror. Its form was human; it gleamed in the dark as white as snow; and when it began to ascend, as dumb as a spirit, to the surface of the earth, Hugues, unable any longer to combat his feelings, turned tail without disguise, and fled.

The footsteps of the phantom pursued him for some time, lending preternatural swiftness to his; but at length, conquering what might after all have been but imagination, he arrived alone at the corner of the forest, deposited the bundle upon the perpendicular stone, and sank fainting at its base.

When he opened his eyes again, startled into life by the howling of the wolves, his hairs stood up one by one upon his head, and cold drops of sweat beaded his brow, as he saw his master standing stark naked before him. The phantom (for such it seemed) seized hold of the bundle, and undoing the knots, dressed himself quietly in the clothes, and bestowing a hearty kick upon the squire—

"And thou, too!" he cried—"thou too must needs be in the cabal! Thou must skip, thou must fly, with a murrain on thy heels! as if there was no other place for a Christian knight to dress in than this accursed corner, with its upright stone of detestable memory!"

"As God is my judge," said Hugues, "it was not from thee I fled! I thought thou wert a loup-garou, and I came hither with thy clothes, of which some villainous treason had despoiled thee. But who, in the name of the Virgin, could have dreamed of seeing thee rising from the earth like a spirit—and from thy own ground too—and as naked as thou wert born!"

"When sawest thou the monk Bonaventure?" asked the knight.

"This afternoon," replied Hugues; "but if he said true, he is by this time in the castle consoling thy disconsolate widow." The knight ground his teeth, and tearing down a branch from a tree, walked with huge strides towards the castle. The noise he made at the gate speedily roused the servants, who were by this time asleep; but in their surprise and confusion, and joy, so long a time elapsed before admittance was afforded, that the birds their master sought were flown.

The Dame of Keridreux, as the history relates, betook herself, Latin, monk, and all, to a far country;

and the knight, after mourning a reasonable time for his loss, went forth again to the wooing, this time successful, of the fair Beatrix.

Father Etienne, on one pretext and another, declined farther intermeddling in the spiritual concerns of so dangerous a family; and Hugues, who could not get the affair of the bundle out of his head, was not sorry for it.

This faithful factotum waxed daily in the good graces of both master and mistress; and when the knight, after supper, would relate the story of his translation into a loup-garou, Hugues as regularly took up the thread of the relation at the passages where he came in himself as a witness.

As for the truth of the stories so related and so confirmed, it is presumed there can be only one opinion. It need not be concealed, however, that some have supposed the supernatural adventure of the knight to have taken place either in his own imagination or by the frolicsome agency of his neighbours; and that his final resumption of his clothes was not really made in the character of a loup-garou, but in that of a self-delivered man who had been incarcerated in the dungeons of his own castle by the fraud and force of a rascally priest and a faithless wife.

But these questions are left to the sagacity of the reader.

CATHERINE CROWE
(1803-1876)

Φ

A Story of a Weir-Wolf

Catherine Crowe is the only female author in this compilation of the best werewolf short stories from 1800-1849. She wrote a few novels, with "Susan Hopley" being her most popular. Yet it is Crowe's supernatural short stories for which she is remembered today.

Two years after "A Story of a Weir-Wolf" appeared in the May 16th, 1846 (Vol. III) issue of James Hogg's magazine *Hogg's Weekly Instructor*, Crowe published "The Night-Side of Nature, or Ghosts and Ghost-seers." The later is a solid compilation of supernatural short stories. Unfortunately, this tale of the weir-wolf that begins "on a fine bright summer's morning" was not contained in "The Night-Side of Nature" and was apparently never re-published by Crowe.

Thankfully the story will live on. Like any good werewolf, it shapeshifted. In 1876—the year of Crowe's death—William Forster produced a play called "The Weirwolf: A Tragedy" that he made clear was "from a story by Mrs. Crowe" in the printed script.

Before you is the complete text of the original short story, which, like a number of others in this collection, is set in the Middle Ages. Like "The Man Wolf," I am unable to find the following tale collected in any anthology.

A Story of a Weir-Wolf

I T WAS on a fine bright summer's morning, in the year 1596, that two young girls were seen sitting at the door of a pretty cottage, in a small village that lay buried amidst the mountains of Auvergne. The house belonged to Ludovique Thierry, a tolerably prosperous builder; one of the girls was his daughter Manon, and the other his niece, Francoise, the daughter of his brother-in-law, Michael Thilouze, a physician.

The mother of Francoise had been some years dead, and Michael, a strange old man, learned in all the mystical lore of the middle ages, had educated his daughter after his own fancy; teaching her some things useless and futile, but others beautiful and true. He not only instructed her to glean information from books, but he led her into the fields, taught her to name each herb and flower, making her acquainted with their properties; and, directing her attention 'to the brave o'erhanging firmament,' he had told her all that was known of the golden spheres that were rolling above her head.

But Michael was also an alchemist, and he had for years been wasting his health in nightly vigils over crucibles,[1] and his means in expensive experiments; and now, alas! he was nearly seventy years of age, and his lovely Francoise seventeen, and neither the *elixir vitæ*[2] nor the philosopher's stone[3] had yet

---

[1] Metal containers
[2] Potion of life
[3] Mythical stone that turns common metals into gold

rewarded his labours. It was just at this crisis, when his means were failing and his hopes expiring, that he received a letter from Paris, informing him that the grand secret was at length discovered by an Italian, who had lately arrived there. Upon this intelligence, Michael thought the most prudent thing he could do was to waste no more time and money by groping in the dark himself, but to have recourse to the fountain of light at once; so sending Francoise to spend the interval with her cousin Manon, he himself started for Paris to visit the successful philosopher.

Although she sincerely loved her father, the change was by no means unpleasant to Francoise. The village of Loques, in which Manon resided, humble as it was, was yet more cheerful than the lonely dwelling of the physician; and the conversation of the young girl more amusing than the dreamy speculations of the old alchemist. Manon, too, was rather a gainer by her cousin's arrival; for as she held her head a little high, on account of her father being the richest man in the village, she was somewhat nice about admitting the neighbouring damsels to her intimacy; and a visiter so unexceptionable as Francoise was by no means unwelcome. Thus both parties were pleased, and the young girls were anticipating a couple of months of pleasant companionship at the moment we have introduced them to our readers, seated at the front of the cottage.

'The heat of the sun is insupportable, Manon,' said Francoise; 'I really must go in.'

'Do,' said Manon.

'But wont you come in too?' asked Francoise.

'No, I don't mind the heat,' replied the other.

Francoise took up her work and entered the house, but as Manon still remained without, the desire for conversation soon overcame the fear of the heat, and she approached the door again, where, standing partly in the shade, she could continue to discourse.

As nobody appeared disposed to brave the heat but Manon, the little street was both empty and silent, so that the sound of a horse's foot crossing the drawbridge, which stood at the entrance of the village, was heard some time before the animal or his rider were in sight. Francoise put out her head to look in the direction of the sound, and, seeing no one, drew it in again; whilst Marion, after casting an almost imperceptible glance the same way, hung hers over her work, as if very intent on what she was doing; but could Francoise have seen her cousin's face, the blush that first overspread it, and the paleness that succeeded, might have awakened a suspicion that Manon was not exposing her complexion to the sun for nothing.

When the horse drew near, the rider was seen to be a gay and handsome cavalier, attired in the perfection of fashion, whilst the rich embroidery of the small cloak tint hung gracefully over his left shoulder, sparkling in the sun, testified no less than his distinguished air to his high rank and condition. Francoise, who had never seen anything so bright and beautiful before, was so entirely absorbed in contemplating the pleasing spectacle, that forgetting to be shy or to hide her own pretty face, she continued to gaze on him as he approached with dilated eyes and lips apart, wholly unconscious that the surprise was mutual. It was not till she saw him lift his bonnet from his head, and, with a reverential bow, do homage to her charms, that her eye fell and the blood rushed to her young cheek. Involuntarily, she made a step backward; into the passage; but when the horse and his rider had passed the door, she almost as involuntarily resumed her position, and protruded her head to look after him. He too had turned round on his horse and was 'riding with his eyes behind,' and the moment he beheld her he lifted his bonnet again, and then rode slowly forward.

'Upon my word, Mam'selle Francoise,' said Manon, with flushed cheeks and angry eyes, 'this is rather remarkable, I think! I was not aware of your acquaintance with Monsieur de Vardes!'

'With whom?' said Francoise. 'Is that Monsieur de Vardes?'

'To be sure it is,' replied Manon; 'do you pretend to say you did not know it?'

'Indeed, I did not,' answered Francoise. 'I never saw him in my life before.'

'Oh, I dare say,' responded Manon, with an incredulous laugh. 'Do you suppose I'm such a fool as to believe you?'

'What nonsense, Manon! How should I know Monsieur de Vardes? But do tell me about him? Does he live at the Chateau?'

'He has been living there lately,' replied Manon, sulkily.

'And where did he live before?' inquired Francoise.

'He has been travelling, I believe,' said Manon.

This was true. Victor de Vardes had been making the tour of Europe, visiting foreign courts, jousting in tournaments, and winning fair ladies' hearts, and was but now returned to inhabit his father's chateau; who, thinking it high time he should be married, had summoned him home for the purpose of paying his addresses to Clemence de Montmorenci, one of the richest heiresses in France.

Victor, who had left home very young, had been what is commonly called *in love* a dozen times, but his heart had in reality never been touched. His loves had been mere boyish fancies, 'dead ere they were born,' one putting out the fire of another before it had had time to hurt himself or any body else; so that when he heard that he was to marry Clemence de Montmorenci, he felt no aversion to the match, and prepared himself to obey his father's behest without a murmur. On being introduced to the lady, be was by no means struck with her. She appeared amiable, sensible, and gentle; but she was decidedly plain, and dressed ill. Victor felt no disposition whatever to love her; but, on the other hand, he had no dislike to her; and as his heart was unoccupied, he expressed himself perfectly ready to comply with the wishes of his family and hers, by whom this alliance had been arranged from motives of mutual interest and accommodation.

So he commenced his course of love; which consisted in riding daily to the chateau of his intended father-in-law, where, if there was company, and he found amusement, he frequently remained a great part of the morning. Now, it happened that his road lay through the village of Loques, where Manon lived, and happening one day to see her at the door, with the gallantry of a gay cavalier, he had saluted her. Manon, who was fully as vain as she was pretty, liked this homage to her beauty so well that she thereafter never neglected an opportunity of throwing herself in the way of enjoying it; and the salutation thus accidentally begun had, from almost daily repetition, ripened into a sort of silent flirtation. The young count smiled, she blushed and half smiled too; and whilst he in reality thought nothing about her, she had brought herself to believe he was actually in love with her, and that it was for her sake he so often appeared riding past her door.

But, on the present occasion, the sight of Francoise's beautiful face had startled the young man out of his good manners. It is difficult to say why a gentleman, who looks upon the features of one pretty girl with indifference, should be 'frightened from his propriety' by the sight of another, in whom the world in general sees nothing superior; but such is the case, and so it was with Victor. His heart seemed taken by storm; he could not drive the beautiful features from his brain; and although he laughed at himself for being thus enslaved by a low-born beauty, he could not laugh himself out of the impatience he felt to mount his horse and ride back again in the hope of once more beholding her. But this time Manon alone was risible; and although he lingered, and allowed his eyes to wander over the house and glance in at the windows, no vestige of the lovely vision could he descry.

'Perhaps she did not live there—she was probably but a visiter to the other girl?' He would have given the world to ask the question of Manon; but he had never spoken to her, and to commence with such an interrogation was impossible, at least Victor felt it so, for his consciousness already made him shrink from betraying the motives of the inquiry. So he saluted Manon and rode on; but the wandering anxious eyes, the relaxed pace, and the cold salutation, were not lost upon her. Besides, he had returned from the Chateau de Montmorenci before the usual time, and the mortified damsel did not fail to discern the motive of this deviation from his habits.

Manon was such a woman as you might live with well enough as long as you steered clear of her vanity, but once come in collision with that, the strongest passion of her nature, and you aroused a latent venom that was sure to make you smart. Without having ever 'vowed eternal friendship,' or pretending to any remarkable affection, the girls had been hitherto very good friends. Manon was aware that Francoise was possessed of a great deal of knowledge of which she was utterly destitute; but as she did not value the knowledge, and had not the slightest conception of what it was worth, she was not mortified by the want of it nor envious of the advantage; she did not consider that it was one. But in the matter of beauty the case was different. She had always persuaded herself that she was much the handsomer of the two. She had black shining hair and dark flashing eyes; and she honestly thought the soft blue eyes and auburn hair of her cousin tame and ineffective.

But the too evident *saisissement*[4] of the young count had shown her a rival where she had not suspected one, and her vexation was as great as her

---

[4] Emotional attention or thrill

surprise. Then she was so puzzled what to do. If she abstained from sitting at the door herself, she should not see Monsieur de Vardes, and if she did sit there her cousin would assuredly do the same. It was extremely perplexing; but Francoise settled the question by seating herself at the door of her own accord. Seeing this, Manon came too, to watch her, but she was sulky and snappish, and when Victor not only distinguished Francoise as before, but took an opportunity of alighting from his horse to tighten his girths, just opposite the door, she could scarcely control her passion.

It would be tedious to detail how, for the two months that ensued, this sort of silent courtship was carried on. Suffice it to say, that by the end of Francoise's visit to Loques she was in complete possession of Victor's heart, and he of hers, although they had never spoken a word to each other; and when she was summoned home to Cabanis to meet her father, she was completely divided betwixt the joy of once more seeing the dear old man and the grief of losing, as she supposed, all chance of beholding again the first love of her young heart.

But here her fears deceived her. Victor's passion had by this time overcome his diffidence, and he had contrived to learn all he required to know about her from the blacksmith of the village, one day when his horse very opportunely lost a shoe; and as Cabanis was not a great way from the Chateau de Montmorenci, he took an early opportunity of calling on the old physician, under pretence of needing his advice.

At first he did not succeed in seeing Francoise, but perseverance brought him better success; and when they became acquainted, he was as much charmed and surprised by the cultivation of her mind as he had been by the beauty of her person. It was not difficult for Victor to win the heart of the alchemist, for the young man really felt, without having occasion to feign, on interest and curiosity with respect to the occult researches so prevalent at that period; and thus, gradually, larger and larger portions of his time were subtracted from the Chateau de Montmorenci to be spent at the physician's. Then, in the green glades of that wide domain which extended many miles around, Victor and Francoise strolled together arm in arm; he vowing eternal affection, and declaring that this rich inheritance of the Montmorenci should never tempt him to forswear his love.

But though thus happy, 'the world forgetting,' they were not 'by the world forgot.' From the day of Victor's first salutation to Francoise, Manon had become her implacable enemy. Her pride made her conceal as much as possible the cause of her aversion; and Francoise, who learned from herself that she had no acquaintance with Victor, hardly knew how to attribute her daily increasing coldness to jealousy. But by the time they parted the alienation was complete, and as, after Francoise went home, all communication ceased between them, it was some time before Manon heard of Victor's visits to Cabanis. But this blissful ignorance was not destined to continue.

There was a young man in the service of the Montmorenci family called Jacques Renard; he was a great favourite with the marquis,[5] who had undertaken to provide for him, when in his early years he was left destitute by the death of his parents, who were old tenants on the estate. Jacques, now filling the office of private secretary to his patron, was extremely in love with the alchemist's daughter; and Francoise, who had seen too little of the world to have much discrimination, had not wholly discouraged his advances. Her heart, in fact, was quite untouched; but very young girls do not know their own hearts; and when Francoise became acquainted with Victor de Vardes, she first

[5] Nobleman who ranks above a count

learned what love is, and made the discovery that she entertained no such sentiment for Jacques Renard. The small encouragement she had given him was therefore withdrawn, to the extreme mortification of the disappointed suitor, who naturally suspected a rival, and was extremely curious to learn who that rival could be; nor was it long before he obtained the information he desired.

Though Francoise and her lover cautiously kept far away from that part of the estate which was likely to be frequented by the Montmorenci family, and thus avoided any inconvenient reencounter with them, they could not with equal success elude the watchfulness of the foresters attached to the domain; and some time before the heiress or Manon suspected how Victor was passing his time, these men were well aware of the hours the young people spent together, either in the woods or at the alchemist's house, which was on their borders. Now the chief forester, Pierre Bloui, was a suitor for Manon's hand. He was an excellent huntsman, but being a weak, ignorant, ill-mannered fellow, she had a great contempt for him, and had repeatedly declined his proposals. But Pierre, whose dullness rendered his sensibilities little acute, had never been reduced to despair. He knew that his situation rendered him, in a pecuniary point of view, an excellent match, and that old Thierry, Manon's father, was his friend; so he persevered in his attentions, and seldom came into Loques without paying her a visit. It was from him she first learned what was going on at Cabanis.

'Ay,' said Pierre, who had not the slightest suspicion of the jealous feelings he was exciting; 'ay, there'll be a precious blow up by and by, when it comes to the ears of the family! What will the Marquis and the old Count de Vardes say, when they find that, instead of making love to Mam'selle Clemence, he spends all his time with Francoise Thilouze?'

'But is not Mam'selle Clemence angry already that he is not more with her?' inquired Manon.

'I don't know,' replied Pierre; 'but that's what I was thinking of asking Jacques Renard, the first time he comes shooting with me.'

'I'm sure I would not put up with it if I were she!' exclaimed Manon, with a toss of the head; 'and I think you would do very right to mention it to Jacques Renard. Besides, it can come to no good for Francoise; for of course the count would never think of marrying *her*.'

'I don't know that,' answered Pierre; 'Margot, their maid, told me another story.'

'You don't mean that the count is going to marry Francoise Thilouze!' exclaimed Manon, with unfeigned astonishment.

'Margot says he is,' answered Pierre.

'Well, then, all I can say is,' cried Manon, her face crimsoning with passion—'all I can say is, that they must have bewitched him, between them; she and that old conjuror, my uncle!'

'Well, I should not wonder,' said Pierre. 'I've often thought old Michael knew more than he should do.'

Now, Manon in reality entertained no such idea, but under the influence of the evil passions that were raging within her at the moment, she nodded her head as significantly as if she were thoroughly convinced of the fact—in short, as if she knew more than she chose to say; and thus sent away the weak superstitious Pierre possessed with a notion that he lost no time in communicating to his brother huntsmen; nor was it long before Victor's attentions to Francoise were made known to Jacques Renard, accompanied with certain suggestions, that Michael Thilouze and his daughter were perhaps what the Scotch call, *no canny;*[6] a persuasion that the foresters themselves found little difficulty in admitting.

---

[6] Unfortunate or unlucky

In the meanwhile, Clemence de Montmorenci had not been unconscious of Victor's daily declining attentions. He had certainly never pressed his suit with great earnestness; but now he did not press it at all. Never was so lax a lover! But as the alliance was one planned by the parents of the young people, not by the election of their own hearts, she contemplated his alienation with more surprise than pain. The elder members of the two families, however, were far from equally indifferent; and when they learned from the irritated, jealous Jacques Renard the cause of the dereliction, their indignation knew no bounds. It was particularly desirable that the estates of Montmorenci and De Vardes should be united, and that the lowly Francoise Thilouze, the daughter of a poor physician, who probably did not know who his grandfather was, should step in to the place designed for the heiress of a hundred quarterings, and mingle her blood with the pure stream that flowed through the veins of the proud De Vardes, was a thing not to be endured.

The strongest expostulations and representations were first tried with Victor, but in vain. 'He was in love, and pleased with ruin.' These failing, other measures must be resorted to; and as in those days, pride of blood, contempt for the rights of the people, ignorance, and superstition, were at their climax, there was little scruple as to the means, so that the end was accomplished.

It is highly probable that these great people themselves believed in witchcraft; the learned, as well as the ignorant, believed in it at that period; and so unaccountable a perversion of the senses as Victor's admiration of Francoise naturally appeared to persons who could discern no merit unadorned by rank, would seem to justify the worst suspicions; so that when Jacques hinted the notion prevailing amongst the foresters with respect to old Michael and his daughter, the idea was seized on with avidity.

Whether Jacques believed in his own allegation it
is difficult to say; most likely not; but it gratified his
spite and served his turn; and his little scrupulous
nature sought no further. The marquis shook his
head ominously, looked very dignified and very grave,
said that the thing must be investigated, and desired
that the foresters, and those who had the best
opportunities for observation, should keep an
attentive eye on the alchemist and his daughter, and
endeavour to obtain some proof of their malpractices,
whilst he considered what was best to be done in
such an emergency.

The wishes and opinions of the great have at all
times a strange omnipotence; and this influence in
1588 was a great deal more potential than it is now.
No sooner was it known that the Marquis de
Montmorenci and the Count de Vardes entertained
an I'll will against Michael and Francoise, than every
body became suddenly aware of their delinquency,
and proofs of it poured in from all quarters. Amongst
other stories, there was one which sprung from
nobody knew where—probably from some hasty
word, or slight coincidence, which flew like wildfire
amongst the people, and caused an immense
sensation. It was asserted that the Montmorenci
huntsmen had frequently met Victor and Francoise
walking together, in remote parts of the domain; but
that when they drew near, she suddenly changed
herself into a wolf and ran off. It was a favourite trick
of witches to transform themselves into wolves, cats,
and hares, and weir-wolves were the terror of the
rustics: and as just at that period there happened to
be one particularly large wolf, that had almost
miraculously escaped the forester's guns, she was
fixed upon as the representative of the
metamorphosed Francoise.

Whilst this storm had been brewing, the old man,
absorbed in his studies, which had received a fresh
impetus from his late journey to Paris, and the young
girl, wrapt in the entrancing pleasures of a first love,

remained wholly unconscious of the dangers that were gathering around them. Margot, the maid, had indeed not only heard, but had *felt* the effects of the rising prejudice against her employers. When she went to Loques for her weekly marketings, she found herself coldly received by some of her old familiars; whilst by those more friendly, she was seriously advised to separate her fortunes from that of persons addicted to such unholy arts. But Margot, who had nursed Francoise in her infancy, was deaf to their insinuations. She knew what they said was false; and feeling assured that if the young count married her mistress, the calumny would soon die away, she did not choose to disturb the peace of the family, and the smooth current of the courtship, by communicating those disagreeable rumours.

In the mean time, Pierre Bloui, who potently believed 'the mischief that himself had made,' was extremely eager to play some distinguished part in the drama of witch- finding. He knew that he should obtain the favour of his employers if he could bring about the conviction of Francoise; and he also thought that he should gratify his mistress. The source of her enmity he did not know, nor care to inquire; but enmity he perceived there was; and he concluded that the destruction of the object of it would be on agreeable sacrifice to the offended Manon. Moreover, he had no compunction, for the conscience of his superiors was his conscience; and Jacques Renard had so entirely confirmed his belief in the witch story, that his superstitious terrors, as well as his interests, prompted him to take an active part in the affair.

Still he felt some reluctance to shoot the wolf; even could he succeed in so doing, from the thorough conviction that it was in reality not a wolf, but a human being he would be aiming at; but he thought if he could entrap her, it would not only save his own feelings, but answer the purpose much better; and accordingly he placed numerous snares, well baited, in that part of the domain most frequented by the lovers; and expected every day, when he visited them, to find Francoise, either in one shape or the other, fast by the leg. He was for some time disappointed; but at length he found in one of the traps, not the wolf or Francoise, but a wolf's foot. An animal had evidently been caught, and in the violence of its struggles for freedom had left its foot behind it. Pierre carried away the foot and baited his trap again.

About a week had elapsed since the occurrence of this circumstance, when one of the servants of the chateau, having met with a slight accident, went to the apothecary's[7] at Loques, for the purpose of purchasing some medicaments; and there met Margot, who had arrived from Cabanis for the same purpose. Mam'selle Francoise, it appeared, had so seriously hurt one of her hands, that her father had been under the necessity of amputating it. As all gossip about the Thilouze family was just then very acceptable at home, the man did not fail to relate what he had heard; and the news, ere long, reached the ears of Pierre Bloui.

It would have been difficult to decide whether horror or triumph prevailed in the countenance of the astonished huntsman at this communication. His face first flushed with joy, and then became pale with affright. It was thus all true! The thing was clear, and he the man destined to produce the proof! It *had* been Francoise that was caught in the trap; and she had released herself at the expense of one of her hands, which, divided from herself, was no longer under the power of her incantations; and had therefore retained the form she had given it, when she resumed her own.

Here was a discovery! Pierre Bloui actually felt himself so overwhelmed by its magnitude, that he

---

[7] Druggist

was obliged to swallow a glass of cogniac[8] to restore his equilibrium, before he could present himself before Jacques Renard to detail this stupendous mystery and exhibit the wolf's foot.

How much Jacques Renard, or the marquis, when he heard it, believed of this strange story, can never be known. Certain it is, however, that within a few hours after this communication had been made to them, the *commissaire du quartier,* followed by a mob from Loques, arrived at Cabanis, and straightway carried away Michael Thilouze and his daughter, on a charge of witchcraft. The influence of their powerful enemies hurried on the judicial process, by courtesy called a trial, where the advantages were all on one side, and the disadvantages all on the other, and poor, terrified, and unaided, the physician and his daughter were, with little delay, found guilty, and condemned to die at the stake. In vain they pleaded their innocence; the wolf's foot was produced in court, and, combined with the circumstance that Francoise Thilouze had really lost her left hand, was considered evidence incontrovertible.

But where was her lover the while? Alas, he was in Paris, where, shortly before these late events, his father had on some pretext sent him; the real object being to remove him from the neighbourhood of Cabanis.

Now, when Manon saw the fruits of her folly and spite, she became extremely sorry for what she had done, for she knew very well that it was with herself the report had originated. But though powerful to harm, she was weak to save. When she found that her uncle and cousin were to lose their lives and die a dreadful death on account of the idle words dropped from her own foolish tongue, her remorse became agonising. But what could she do? Where look for assistance? Nowhere, unless in Victor de Vardes, and he was far away. She had no jealousy

---

[8] French brandy

now; glad, glad would she have been, to be preparing to witness her cousin's wedding instead of her execution! But those were not the days of fleet posts—if they had been, Manon would have doubtless known how to write.

As it was, she could neither write a letter to the count, nor have sent it when written. And yet, in Victor lay her only hope. In this trait she summoned Pierre Bloui, and asked him if he would go to Paris for her, and inform the young count of the impending misfortune. But it was not easy to persuade Pierre to so rash an enterprise. He was afraid of bringing himself into trouble with the Montmorencis. But Manon's heart was in the cause. She represented to him, that if he lost one employer he would get another, for that the young count would assuredly become his best friend; and when she found that this was not enough to win him to her purpose, she bravely resolved to sacrifice herself to save her friends.

'If you will hasten to Paris,' she said, 'stopping neither night nor day, and tell Monsieur de Vardes of the danger my uncle and cousin are in, when you come back I will marry you.'

The bribe succeeded, and Pierre consented to go, owning that he was the more willing to do so, because he had privately changed his own opinion with respect to the guilt of the accused parties. 'For,' said he, 'I saw the wolf last night under the chestnut trees, and as she was very lame, I could have shot her, but I feared my lord and lady would be displeased.'

'Then, how can you be foolish enough to think it's my cousin,' said Manon, 'when you know she is in prison?'

'That's what I said to Jacques Renard,' replied Pierre; 'but he bade me not meddle with what did not concern me.'

In fine, love and conscience triumphed over fear and servility, and as soon as the sun set behind the hills, Pierre Bloui started for Paris.

How eagerly now did Manon reckon the days and hours that were to elapse before Victor could arrive. She had so imperfect an idea of the distance to be traversed, that after the third day she began hourly to expect him; but sun after sun rose and set, and no Victor appeared; and in the mean time, before the very windows of the house she dwelt in, she beheld preparations making day by day for the fatal ceremony. From early morn to dewy eve, the voices of the workmen, the hammering of the scaffolding, and the hum of the curious and excited spectators, who watched its progress, resounded in the ears of the unhappy Manon; for a witch-burning was a sort of *auto da fe*,[9] like the burning of a heretic, and was anticipated as a grand spectacle, alike pleasing to gods and men, especially in the little town of Loques, where exciting scenes of any kind were very rare.

Thus time crept on, and still no signs of rescue; whilst the anguish and remorse of the repentant sinner became unbearable.

Now, Manon was not only a girl of strong passions but of a fearless spirit. Indeed the latter was somewhat the offspring of the former; for when her feelings were excited, not only justice and charity, as we have seen, were apt to be forgotten, but personal danger and feminine fears were equally overlooked in the tempest that assailed her. On the present occasion, her better feelings were in full activity. Her whole nature was aroused, self was not thought of, and to save the lives she had endangered by her folly, she would have gladly laid down her own. 'For why live,' thought she, 'if my uncle and cousin die? I can never be happy again; besides, I must keep my promise and marry Pierre Bloui; and I had better lose

---

[9] Act of religious faith

my life in trying to expiate my fault than live to be miserable.'

Manon had a brother called Alexis, who was now at the wars; often and often, in this great strait, she had wished him at home; for she knew that he would have undertaken the mission to Paris for her, and so have saved her the sacrifice she had made in order to win Pierre to her purpose. Now, when Alexis lived at home, and the feuds between the king and the grand seigneurs[10] had brought the battle to the very doors of the peasants of Auvergne, Manon had many a time braved danger in order to bring this much loved brother refreshments on his night watch; and he had, moreover, as an accomplishment which might be some time needed for her own defence, taught her to carry a gun and shoot at a mark.

In those days of civil broil and bloodshed, country maidens were not unfrequently adept in such exercises. This acquirement she now determined to make available; and when the eve of the day appointed for the execution arrived without any tidings from Paris, she prepared to put her plan in practice. This was no other than to shoot the wolf herself, and, by producing it, to prove the falsity of the accusation. For this purpose, she provided herself with a young pig, which she slung in a sack over her shoulder, and with her brother's gun on the other, and disguised in his habiliments, when the shadows of twilight fell upon the earth, the brave girl went forth into the forest on her bold enterprise alone.

She knew that the moon would rise ere she reached her destination, and on this she reckoned for success. With a beating heart she traversed the broad glades, and crept through the narrow paths that intersected the wide woods till she reached the chestnut avenue where Pierre said he had seen the lame wolf. She was aware that old or disabled

---

[10] Feudal lord

animals, who are rendered unfit to hunt their prey, will be attracted a long distance by the scent of food; so having hung her sack with the pig in it to the lower branch of a tree, she herself ascended another close to it, and then presenting the muzzle of her gun straight in the direction of the bag, she sat still as a statue; and there, for the present, we must leave her, whilst we take a peep into the prison of Loques, and see how the unfortunate victims of malice and superstition are supporting their captivity and prospect of approaching death.

Poor Michael Thilouze and his daughter had had a rude awakening from the joyous dreams in which they had both been wrapt. The old man's journey to Paris had led to what he believed would prove the most glorious results. It was true that report had as usual exaggerated the success of his fellow labourer there. The Italian Alascer had not actually found the philosopher's stone—but he was on the eve of finding it—one single obstacle stood in his way, and had for a considerable time arrested his progress; and as he was an old man, worn out by anxious thought and unremitting labour, who could scarcely hope to enjoy his own discovery, he consented to disclose to Michael not only all he knew, but also what was the insurmountable difficulty that had delayed his triumph. This precious stone, he had ascertained, which was not only to ensure to the fortunate possessor illimitable wealth, but perennial youth, could not be procured without the aid of a virgin, innocent, perfect, and pure; and, moreover, capable of inviolably keeping the secret which must necessarily be imparted to her.

'Now,' said the Italian, 'virgins are to be had in plenty; but the second condition I find it impossible to fulfill; for they invariably confide what I tell them to some friend or lover; and thus the whole process becomes vitiated, and I am arrested on the very threshold of success.'

Great was the joy of Michael on hearing this; for he well knew that Francoise, his pure, innocent, beautiful Francoise, *could* keep a secret; he had often had occasion to prove her fidelity; so bidding the Italian keep himself alive but for a little space, when he, in gratitude for what he had taught him, would return with the long sought for treasure, and restore him to health, wealth, and vigorous youth, the glad old man hurried back to Cabanis, and 'set himself about it like the sea.'

It was in performing the operation required of her that Francoise had so injured her hand that amputation had become unavoidable; and great as had been the joy of Michael was now his grief. Not only had his beloved daughter lost her hand, but the hopes he had built on her co-operation were forever annihilated; maimed and dismembered, she was no longer eligible to assist in the sublime process. But how much greater was his despair, when he learned the suspicions to which this strange coincidence had subjected her, and beheld the innocent, and till now happy girl, led by his side to a dungeon. For himself he cared nothing; for her everything. He was old and disappointed, and to die was little to him—but his Francoise, his young and beautiful Francoise, cut off in her bloom of years, and by so cruel and ignominious a death! And here they were in prison alone, helpless and forsaken! Absorbed in his studies, the poor physician had lived a solitary life; and his daughter, holding a rank a little above the peasantry and below the gentry, had had no companion but Manon, and she was now her bitterest foe; this at least they were told.

How sadly and slowly, and yet how much too fleetly, passed the days that were to intervene betwixt the sentence and the execution. And where was Victor? Where were his vows of love and eternal faith? All, all forgotten. So thought Francoise, who, ignorant of his absence from the Chateau de Vardes, supposed him well acquainted with her distress.

Thus believing themselves abandoned by the world, the poor father and daughter, in tears, and prayers, and attempts at mutual consolation, spent this sad interval, till at length the morning dawned that was to witness the us accomplishment of their dreadful fate. During the preceding night old Michael had never closed his eyes; but Francoise had fallen asleep shortly before sunrise, and was dreaming that it was her wedding day; and that, followed by the cheers of the villagers, Victor, the still beloved Victor, was leading her to the altar. The cheers awoke her, and with the smile of joy still upon her lips, she turned her face to her father. He was stretched upon the floor overcome by a burst of uncontrollable anguish at the sounds that had aroused her from her slumbers; for the sounds were real. The voices of the populace, crowding in from the adjacent country and villages to witness the spectacle, had pierced the thick walls of the prison and reached the cars and the hearts of the captives. Whilst the old man threw himself at her feet, and, pouring blessings on her fair young head, besought her pardon, Francoise almost forgot her own misery in his; and when the assistants came to lead them forth to execution, she not only exhorted him to patience, but supported with her arm the feeble frame that, wasted by age and grief, could furnish but little fuel for the flame that awaited them.

Nobody would have imagined that in this thinly peopled neighbourhood so many persons could have been brought together as were assembled in the marketplace of Loques to witness the deaths of Michael Thilouze and his daughter. A scaffolding had been erected all round the square for the spectators—that designed for the gentry being adorned with tapestry and garlands of flowers. There sat, amongst others, the families of Montmorenci and De Vardes—all except the Lady Clemence, whose heart recoiled from beholding the death of her rival; although, no more enlightened than her age, she did not doubt the justice of the sentence that had condemned her. In the centre of the area was a pile of faggots, and near it stood the assistant executioners and several members of the church— priests and friars in their robes of black and grey.

The prisoners, accompanied by a procession which was headed by the judge and terminated by the chief executioner of the law, were first marched round the square several times, in order that the whole of the assembly might be gratified with the sight of them; and then being placed in front of the pile, the bishop of the district, who attended in his full canonicals,[11] commenced a mass for the souls of the unhappy persons about to depart this life under such painful circumstances, after which he pronounced a somewhat lengthy oration on the enormity of their crime, ending with an exhortation to confession and repentance.

These, which constituted the whole of the preliminary ceremonies, being concluded, and the judge having read the sentence, to the effect, that, being found guilty of abominable and devilish magic arts, Michael and Francoise Thilouze were condemned to be burnt, especially for that the said Francoise, by her own arts, and those of her father, had bewitched the Count Victor de Vardes, and had sundry times visibly transformed herself into the shape of a wolf, and being caught in a trap, had thereby lost her hand, &c., the prisoners were delivered to the executioner, who prepared to bind them previously to their being placed on the pile. Then Michael fell upon his knees, and crying aloud to the multitude, besought them to spare his daughter, and to let him die alone; and the hearts of some amongst the people were moved. But from that part of the area where the nobility were seated, there issued a voice of authority, bidding the executioner proceed; so the old man and the young girl were

---

[11] Religious clothing with Bible

placed upon the pile, and the assistants, with torches in their hands, drew near to set it alight, when a murmur arose from afar, then a hum of voices, a movement in the assembled crowd, which began to sway to and fro like the awing of vast waters.

Then there was a cry of 'Make way! make way! open a path! let her advance!' and the crowd divided, and a path was opened, and there came forward, slowly and with difficulty pie, disheveled, with clothes torn and stained with blood Manon Thierry, dragging behind her a dead wolf. The crowd closed in as she advanced, and when she reached the centre of the arena, there was straightway a dead silence. She stood for a moment looking around, and when she saw where the persons in authority sat, she fell upon her knees and essayed to speak; but her voice was choked by emotion, no word escaped her lips; she could only point to the wolf, and plead for mercy by her looks; where her present anguish of soul, and the danger and terror she had lately encountered, were legibly engraved.

The appeal was understood, and gradually the voices of the people rose again—there was a reaction. They who had been so eager for the spectacle, were now ready to supplicate for the victims—the young girl's heroism had conquered their sympathies. 'Pardon! pardon!' was the cry, and a hope awoke in the hearts of the captives. But the interest of the Montmorencis was too strong for that of the populace—the nobility stood by their order, and stern voices commanded silence, and that the ceremony should proceed; and once more the assistants brandished their torches and advanced to the pile; and then Manon, exhausted with grief, terror, and loss of blood, fell upon her face to the ground.

But now, again, there is a sound from afar, and all voices are hushed, and all ears are strained—it is the echo of a horse's foot galloping over the drawbridge;

it approaches; and again, like the surface of a stormy sea, the dense crowd is in motion; and then a path is opened, and a horse, covered with foam, is seen advancing, and thousands of voices burst forth into 'Viva! Viva!' The air rings with acclamations. The rider was Victor de Vardes, bearing in his hand the king's order for arrest of execution.

Pierre Bloui had faithfully performed his embassy; and the brave Henry IV., moved by the prayers and representations of the ardent lover, had hastily furnished him with a mandate commanding respite till further investigation.

Kings were all-powerful in those days; and it was no sooner known that Henry was favourable to the lovers, than the harmlessness of Michael and his daughter was generally acknowledged; the production of the wolf wanting a foot being now considered as satisfactory a proof of their innocence, as the production of the foot wanting the wolf had formerly been of their guilt.

Strange human passions, subject to such excesses and to such revulsions! Michael Thilouze and his daughter happily escaped; and under the king's countenance and protection, the young couple were married; but we need not remind such of our readers as are learned in the annals of witchcraft, how many unfortunate persons have died at the stake for crimes imputed to them, on no better evidence than this.

As for the heiress of Montmorenci, she bore her loss with considerable philosophy. She would have married the young Count de Vardes without repugnance, but he had been too cold a lover to touch her heart or occasion regret; but poor Manon was the sacrifice for her own error. What manner of contest she had had with the wolf was never known, for she never sufficiently recovered from the state of exhaustion in which she had fallen to the earth, to be able to describe what had passed. Alone she had vanquished the savage animal, alone dragged it through the forest and the village, to the market square, where every human being able to stir, for miles round, was assembled; so that all other places were wholly deserted. The wolf had been shot, but not mortally; its death had evidently been accelerated by other wounds. Manon herself was much torn and lacerated; and on the spot where the creature had apparently been slain, was found her gun, a knife, and a pool of blood, in which lay several fragments of her dress: Though unable to give any connected account of her own perilous adventure, she was conscious of the happy result of her generous devotion; and before she died received the heartfelt forgiveness and earnest thanks of her uncle and cousin, the former of whom soon followed her to the grave. Despairing now of ever succeeding in his darling object, what was the world to him! He loved his daughter tenderly, but he was possessed with an idea, which it had been the aim and hope of his life to work out. She was safe and happy, and needed him no more; and the hope being dead, life seemed to ooze out with it.

By the loss of that maiden's hand, who can tell what we have missed! For doubtless it is the difficulty of fulfilling the last condition named by the Italian, which has been the real impediment in the way of all philosophers who have been engaged in alchemical pursuits; and we may reasonably hope, that when women shall have learned to hold their tongues, the philosopher's stone will be discovered, and poverty and wrinkles thereafter cease to deform the earth.

For long years after these strange events, over the portcullis[12] of the old chateau of the De Vardes, till it fell into utter ruin, might be discerned the figure of a wolf, carved in stone, wanting one of its fore-feet; and

---

[12] Iron gate

underneath   it   the   following   inscription—'*In
perpetuam rei memoriam.*'[13]

---

[13] In everlasting remembrance.

RICHARD THOMSOM
(1794-1865)

Φ

The Wehr-Wolf
A Legend of the Limousin

This excellent tale of the werewolf came to light in the February 23, 1828, Vol. I issue of *The Olio, or, Museum of Entertainment*. It appeared on page 97 below an illustration of knights fighting on the battlefield. The story was first published anonymously. It next appeared when Richard Thomson published his three volume collection of short stories called, "Tales of an Antiquary." In Vol. I is "The Wehr-Wolf: A Legend of the Limousin." Thomson was librarian of the London Institute and a historian. His collection melded history and fiction in the way one would expect from a person with his literary background.

The story made such an impression that an 1828 Playbill for the Pavilion Theatre of London reveals a production titled: "The Wehr Wolf, or, The Hunter of Limousin" that same year. The playwright is listed as J. G. Reynolds.

This is the oldest werewolf story in this collection and one of the best. It forms the foundation of the modern werewolf short story on which the others were built. At a minimum, it must be praised for its originality. The story provides the first concept I have found in the literature of wearing a werewolf skin as a cloak to prevent attacks from other werewolves and animals. It also is apparently the first to describe the concept of striking a man beset with werewolfism between the eyes with a "fire fork" to change him back into the beast. It even has some comedic moments as did the play, which contained a comic song titled "Billy Barlow."

The setting of the story is 1520.

The Wehr-Wolf
A Legend of the Limousin

The Wolf! the Wolf!
Æsop's Fables

'TWAS SMOOTHLY SAID, IN OLDEN HOURS,
THAT MEN WERE OFT WITH WONDROUS POWERS,
ENDOW'D THEIR WONTED FORMS TO CHANGE,
AND WEHR-WOLVES WILD ABROAD TO RANGE!
SO GARWAL ROAMS IN SAVAGE PRIDE,
   AND HUNTS FOR BLOOD AND FEEDS ON MEN,
SPREADS DIRE DESTRUCTION FAR AND WIDE,
   AND MAKES THE FORESTS BROAD HIS DEN.
MARIE'S "LAI DU BISCLAVARET."

THE ancient Province of Poictou, in France, has long been celebrated in the annals of Romance, as one of the most famous haunts of those dreadful animals, whose species is between a phantom and a beast of prey; and which are called by the Germans, Wehr-Wolves, and by the French, Bisclavarets, or Loups Garoux. To the English, these midnight terrors are yet unknown, and almost without a name; but when they are spoken of in this country, they are called by way of eminence, Wild Wolves!

The common superstition concerning them is, that they are men in compact with the Arch Enemy, who have the power of assuming the form and nature of wolves at certain periods. The hilly and woody district of the Upper Limousin, which now forms the Southern division of the Upper Vienne, was that particular part of the Province which the Wehr-Wolves were supposed to inhabit; whence, like the animals which gave them their name, they would wander out by midnight, far from their own hills and mountains, and run howling through the silent streets of the nearest towns and villages, to the great terror of all the inhabitants; whose piety, however, was somewhat increased by these supernatural visitations.

There once stood in the suburbs of the Town of St. Yrieux, which is situate in those dangerous parts of ancient Poictou, an old, but handsome, *Maison-de-Plaisance*, or, in plain English, a country-house, belonging by ancient descent to the young Baroness Louise Joliedame; who, out of a dread of the terrible Wehr-Wolves, a well-bred horror at the *chambres à l'antique*[1] which it contained, and a greater love for the gallant Court of Francis I., let the Chateau to strangers; though they occupied but a very small portion of it, whilst the rest was left unrepaired, and was rapidly falling to decay.

One of the parties by whom the old mansion was tenanted, was a country Chirurgeon,[2] named Antoine Du Pilon; who, according to his own account, was not only well acquainted with the science of Galen[3] and Hippocrates,[4] but was also a profound adept in those arts, for the learning of which some men toil their whole lives away, and are none the wiser; such as Alchemy,[5] converse with spirits, Magic, and so forth.

Dr. Du Pilon had abundant leisure to talk of his knowledge at the little Cabaret[6] of St. Yrieux, which

---

[1] Ancient rooms
[2] Antiquate Middle English term for surgeon
[3] Claudius Galenus (129-217), popular Roman physician
[4] Hippocrates of Cos (460 B.C. – 370 B.C.), ancient Greek physician
[5] Pseudo-science of converting base metals to gold
[6] Social gathering place

bore the sign of the Chevalier Bayard's Arms,[7] where he assembled round him many of the idler members of the town, the chief of whom were Cuirbouilli, the Currier;[8] Malbois, the Joiner;[9] La Jacquette, the Tailor, and Nicole Bonvarlet, his Host, together with several other equally arrant gossips, who all swore roundly, at the end of each of their parleys, that Doctor Antoine du Pilon was the best Doctor, and the wisest man in the whole world!

To remove, however, any wonder that may arise in the reader's mind, how a professor of such skill and knowledge should be left to waste his abilities so remote from the patronage of the great, it should be remarked, that in such cases as had already come before him, he had not been quite so successful as could have been expected, or desired; since old Genifréde Corbeau, who was frozen almost double with age and ague,[10] he kept cold and fasting, to preserve her from fever; and he would have cut off the leg of Pierre Faucille, the reaper, when he wounded his right arm in harvest time, to prevent the flesh from mortifying downwards!

In a retired apartment of the same deserted mansion where this mirror of Chirurgeons resided, dwelt a peasant and his daughter, who had come to St. Yrieux from a distant part of Normandy, and of whose history nothing was known, but that they seemed to be in the deepest poverty; although they neither asked relief, nor uttered a single complaint. Indeed they rather avoided all discourse with their gossiping neighbours, and even with their fellow inmates, excepting so far as the briefest courtesy required; and as they were able, on entering their abode, to place a reasonable security for payment in

---

[7] Crest of Chevalier de Bayard (1473-1524), reputed to be the last true knight and perhaps the person on which the protagonist of Miguel de Cervantes's (1547-1616) famous book: "Don Quixote" is based.

[8] Leather tanner

[9] Woodworker who fits joints together without the use of nails

[10] Off-and-on fever marked by chills

the hands of old Gervais, the Baroness Joliedame's Steward, they were permitted to live in the old Chateau with little questioning, and less sympathy.

The father appeared in general to be a plain rude peasant, whom poverty had somewhat tinctured with misanthropy; though there were times when his bluntness towered into a haughtiness not accordant with his present station, but seemed like a relique of a higher sphere from which he had fallen. He strove, and the very endeavour increased the bitterness of his heart to mankind, to conceal his abject indigence, but that was too apparent to all, since he was rarely to be found at St. Yrieux, but led a wild life in the adjacent mountains and forests, occasionally visiting the town, to bring to his daughter Adéle a portion of the spoil, which, as a hunter, he indefatigably sought for the subsistence of both. Adéle, on the contrary, though she felt as deeply as her father the sad reverse of fortune to which they were exposed, had more gentleness in her sorrow, and more content in her humiliation. She would, when he returned to the cottage, worn with the fatigue of his forest labours, try, but many times in vain, to bring a smile to his face, and consolations to his heart. "My father," she would say, "quit, I beseech you, this wearisome hunting for some safer employment, nearer home. You depart, and I watch in vain for your return; days and nights pass away, and you come not! while my disturbed imagination will ever whisper the danger of a forest midnight, fierce, howling wolves, and robbers still more cruel."

"Robbers! girl, sayest thou?" answered her *father* with a bitter laugh, "and what shall they gain from me, think ye? is there aught in this worn-out gaberdine[11] to tempt them? Go to, Adéle! I am not now Count Gaspar de Marcanville, the friend of the royal Francis, and a Knight of the Holy Ghost; but

---

[11] Cheap and worn overcoat

plain Hubert, the Hunter of the Limousin; and wolves, thou trowest, will not prey upon wolves."

"But, dear my father," said Adéle, embracing him, "I would that thou would'st seek a safer occupation nearer to our dwelling, for I would be by your side."

"What would'st have me to do, girl?" interrupted Gaspar impatiently; "would'st have me put this hand to the sickle, or the plough, which has so often grasped a sword in the battle, and a banner-lance in the tournament? or shall a companion of Le Saint-Esprit become a fellow-handworker with the low artizans of this miserable town? I tell thee Adéle, that but for thy sake I would never again quit the forest, but would remain there in a savage life, till I forgot my language and my species, and became a Wehr-wolf, or a wild-buck!"

Such was commonly the close of their conversation; for if Adéle dared to press her entreaties farther, Gaspar, half frenzied, would not fail to call to her mind all the unhappy circumstances of his fall, and work himself almost to madness by their repetition. He had in early life been introduced by the Count De Saintefleur to the Court of Francis I., where he had risen so high in the favour of his Sovereign, that he was continually in his society; and in the many wars which so embittered the reign of that excellent Monarch, De Marcanville's station was ever by his side.

In these conflicts, Gaspar's bosom had often been the shield of Francis, even in moments of the most imminent danger; and the grateful King as often showered upon his deliverer those rewards, which, to the valiant and high-minded soldier, are far dearer than riches; the glittering jewels of knighthood, and the golden coronal of the peerage. To that friend who had fixed his feet so loftily and securely in the slippery paths of a Court, Gaspar felt all the ardour of youthful gratitude; and yet he sometimes imagined, that he could perceive an abatement in the favour of De Saintefleur, as that of Francis increased.

The truth was, that the gold and rich promises of the King's great enemy, the Emperor Charles V., had induced De Saintefleur to swerve from his allegiance; and he now waited but for a convenient season to put the darkest designs in practice against his Sovereign. He also felt no slight degree of envy, even against that very person whom he had been the instrument of raising; and at length an opportunity occurred, when he might gratify both his ambition and his revenge, by the same blow. It was in one of those long wars in which the French Monarch was engaged, and in which De Saintefleur and De Marcanville were his most constant companions, that they were both watching near his couch whilst he slept, when the former, in a low tone of voice, thus began to sound the faith of the latter towards his royal master.

"What say'st thou, Gaspar, were not a prince's coronet and a king's revenue in Naples, better than thus ever toiling in a war that seems unending? Hearest thou, brave De Marcanville? we can close it with the loss of one life only!"

"Queen of Heaven!" ejaculated Gaspar, "what is it thou would'st say, De Saintefleur?"

"Say! why that there have been other Kings of France before this Francis, and will be, when he shall have gone to his place. Thinkest thou that He of the double-headed black eagle would not amply reward the sword that cut this fading lily from the earth?"

"No more, no more, De Saintefleur!" cried Gaspar; "even from you, who placed me where I might flourish beneath that lily's shade, will I not hear this treason. Rest secure that I will not betray thee to the King; my life shall sooner be given for thine; but I will watch thee with more vigilance than the wolf hath when he watcheth the night-fold, and your first step to the heart of Francis shall be over the body of Gaspar De Marcanville."

"Nay, then," said De Saintefleur aside, "he must be my first victim," and immediately drawing his sword, he cried aloud, "What, ho! guards! Treason!"—whilst Gaspar stood immoveable with astonishment and horror. The event is soon related, for Francis was but too easily persuaded that De Marcanville was in reality guilty of the act about to have been perpetrated by De Saintefleur; and the magnanimity of Gaspar was such, that not one word which might criminate his former friend could be drawn from him, even to save his own life. The kindhearted Francis, however, was unable to forget in a moment the favour with which for years he had been accustomed to look upon De Marcanville; and it was only at the earnest solicitation of the Courtiers,[12] many of whom were rejoiced at the thought of a powerful rival's removal, that he could be prevailed on to pass upon him even the sentence of degradation and banishment.

Gaspar hastened to his Chateau, but the treasures which he was allowed to bear with him into exile were little more than his Rosalie and his daughter Adéle; with whom he immured himself in the dark and almost boundless recesses of the Hanoverian Harz,[13] where his fatigues and his sorrows soon rendered his gaunt and attenuated form altogether unknown.

In this savage retirement, he drew up a faithful narration of De Saintefleur's treachery; and in confirmation of it's truth, procured a certificate from his Confessor, Father Ægidius,—one of those holy men who of old were dwellers in forests and deserts,—and directing it "To the King," placed it in the hands of his wife, that if, in any of those hazardous excursions in which he engaged to procure their daily subsistence, he should perish, it

[12] Those who attend the royal court and are often advisors to it

[13] Harz mountain range of Germany that is reputed to contain spirits and demons

might be delivered to Francis, and his family thus be restored to their rank and estates, when his pledge to De Saintefleur could no longer be claimed.

Years passed away, and, in the gloomy recesses of the Hercynian woods,[14] Gaspar acquired considerable skill as a hunter: had it been to preserve his own life only, he had laid him calmly down upon the sod, and resigned that life to famine, or to the hungry wolf; but he had still two objects which bound him to existence, and therefore in the chase the wild-buck was too slow to escape his spear, and the bear too weak to resist his attacks.

His fate, notwithstanding, preyed heavily upon him, and often brake out in fits of vehement passion, and the most bitter lamentations; which at length so wrought upon the grief-worn frame of Rosalie de Marcanville, that about ten years after Gaspar's exile, her death left him a widower, when his daughter Adéle was scarcely eighteen years of age.

It was then, with a mixture of desperation and distress, that De Marcanville determined to rush forth from his solitude into France, and, careless of the fate which might await him for returning from exile unrecalled, to advance even to the Court, and laying his papers at the foot of the throne, to demand the Ordeal of Combat with De Saintefleur; but when he had arrived at the woody Province of the Upper Limousin, his purpose failed him, as he saw in the broad day-light, which rarely entered the Harz Forest, the afflicting changes which ten years of the severest labour, and the most heartfelt sorrow, had made upon his form. He might, indeed, so far as it regarded all recollections of his person, have safely gone even into the Court of Francis; but Gaspar also saw, that in the retired forest surrounding St. Yrieux, he might still reside unknown in his beloved France; that under the guise of a hunter, he could still

---

[14] Large and dense tract of forest that stretched across German in the Middle Ages and contained the Harz Mountains

provide for the support of his gentle Adéle; and that, in the event of his death, she would be considerably nearer to her Sovereign's abode. It was, then, in consequence of these reasons, that De Marcanville employed a part of his small remaining property, in securing a residence in the dilapidated Chateau, as it has been already mentioned.

It was some time after their arrival, that the inhabitants of the Town of St. Yrieux were alarmed by the intelligence, that a Wehr-Wolf, or perhaps a troop of them, certainly inhabited the woods of the Limousin. The most terrific howlings were heard in the night, and the wild rush of a chase swept through the deserted streets; yet the townspeople— according to the most approved rules for acting where Wehr-Wolves are concerned,—never once thought of sallying forth in a body, and with weapons, and lighted brands, to scare the monsters from their prey; but, adding a more secure fastening to every window, which is the Wehr-Wolf's usual entrance, they deserted such as had already fallen their victims, with one brief expression of pity for *them*, and many a "*Dieu me benit!*"[15] for *themselves*. It was asserted, too, that some of the country people, whose dwellings came more immediately into contact with the Limousin forests, had lost their children, whose lacerated remains, afterwards discovered in the woods, only half devoured, plainly denoted them to have fallen the prey of some abandoned Wehr-Wolf!

It is not surprising, that in a retired town, where half the people were without employment, and all were thorough-bred gossips, and lovers of wonders, that the inroads of the Wehr-Wolves formed too important an epoch in their history, to be passed over without a due discussion. Under pretence, therefore, of being a protection to each other, many of the people of St. Yrieux, and especially the worthy

---

[15] God bless me

conclave mentioned at the beginning of this history, were, almost eternally, convened at the Chevalier Bayard's Arms; talking over their nightly terrors, and filling each other with such affright, by the repetition of many a lying old tale upon the same subject, that, too much alarmed to part, they often agreed to pass the night over Nicole Bonvarlet's wine-flask and blazing fagots. Upon a theme so intimately connected with magical lore as is the history of Wehr-Wolves, Dr. Antoine Du Pilon discoursed like a Solomon;[16] citing, to the great edification and wonder of his hearers, such hosts of authors, both sacred and profane, that he who should but have hinted, that the Wehr-Wolves of St. Yrieux were simply like other Wolves, would have found as little gentleness in his hearers, as he would have experienced from the animals themselves.

"Well, my masters!" began Bonvarlet, one evening when they were met, "I would not, for a tun of malmsey wine[17] now, be in the Limousin forest to-night; for do ye hear how it blusters and pours? By the Ship of St. Mildred![18] in a wild night like this, there's no place in the world like your hearth-side in a goodly auberge, with a merry host and good liquor; both of which, neighbours, ye have to admiration."

"Aye, Nicole," replied Cuirbouilli, "it's a foul night, truly, either for man or cattle; and yet I'll warrant ye that the Wehr-Wolves will be out in't, for their skin is said to be the same as that the Fiend himself wears! and that would shut you out water, and storm, and wind, like a castle-wall. Mass, now! but it would be simply the making of my fortune, an' I could but get one of their hides!"

"Truly, for a churl," began Dr. Du Pilon, "an unlettered artizan, thy wish sheweth a pretty wit; for a cloak made from the skin of a Wehr-Wolf, would for

---

[16] Reference to the wisdom of Biblical Jewish king of the same name

[17] Sweet dessert wine made in Madeira Island off Portugal

[18] Daughter of King Merewald of Magonset, who escaped the machinations of the Abbess of Chelles by ship at night

ever defend it's wearer from all other Wolves, and all animals that your Wolves feed upon: even, as Pythagoras writeth, that one holding the eye of a Wolf in his hand, shall scare away from him all weaker creatures; for like as the sight of a Wolf doth terrify—"

"Hark, neighbours! did ye hear that cry? it is a Wehr-Wolf's bark!" exclaimed Jerome Malbois, starting from his settle.

"Aye, by the Bull of St. Luke![19] did I, friend Jerome," returned Bonvarlet, "surely the great Fiend himself can make no worser a howling; I even thought 'twould split the very rafters last night, though I deem that they're of good seasoned fir."

"There thou errest again," said the Doctor in a pompous tone to the last speaker, "Oh! ye rustics, whom I live with as Orpheus did with the savages of Thracia,[20] whence is it that ye possess such boundless stupidity? Thou sayest, Jerome Malbois, that they bark, and, could I imagine, that shooting in the dark, thou had'st hit on the Greekish phrase which calls them Νυxτεϛι voι Kανεϛ, or Dogs of the Night, I could say thou had said wisely: but now I declare that thou hast spoken full ignorantly, right woodenly, Jerome Malbois; thou art beyond thy square, friend joiner; thou hast overstepped thy rule, good Carpenter. Doth not the great Albertus[21] bear testimony, Oh, most illiterate! that Wolves bark not, when he saith,—

'Ast Lupus ipse *vlulat*, frendit agrestis aper,'

which for thine edification is, in the vulgar tongue,—

---

[19] Religious symbol of Saint Luke, the apostle of Jesus Christ
[20] Orpheus was attacked by the female savages of Thracia and dismembered
[21] Saint Albertus Magnus (1206-1280), who advocated the coexistence of religious doctrines beside scientific principles

But the Wolf doth loudly howl, and the boar his teeth
   doth grind.
Where the wildest plains are spread before, and
   forests rise behind.

Et idem Auctor, and the same Author also saith,
which maketh yet more against thee, O *mentis inops!*

'Per noctem resonare Lupus, *vlulantibus* urbes.'

which in the common is

   The Wolf by night through silent cities prowls,
   And makes the streets resound with hideous
   howls.

And doth not Servius[22] say the like in a verse
wherein I opine he hints at Wehr-Wolves? '*Vlulare,*
canum est furiare'—to howl is the voice of dogs and
furies:—thus findest thou, *Faber sciolus!* that here
we have an agreement touching the voice of wolves,
which is low and mournful, and therefore the word
Vlulatus is fitly applied as an imitation thereof. Your
Almaine[23] says *Heulen;* the Frenchman saith *Hurler;*
and the Englishman, with a conglomeration of
sounds as bad as the Wolf's own, calleth it howling."
   "By the holy Dog of Tobias!"[24] ejaculated Bonvarlet,
"and I think our Doctor speaketh all languages, as he
had had his head broken with a brick from the Tower
of Babel, and all the tongues had got in at once.[25]
But where think ye Monsieur, that these cursed
Loups Garoux came from? Are they like unto other
Wolves, or what breed be they?"

---

[22] Servius Maurus Honoratus, grammarian of the late fourth century
[23] German
[24] Biblical son of Tobit,
[25] Tower of Babel is the Biblical story of the people trying to build a
tower to heaven that God destroyed and caused the people to speak in
different languages for punishment

"Nicole Bonvarlet," again began the untired Doctor, after taking a long draught of the flask, "Nicole Bonvarlet, I perceive thou hast more of good literature than thy fellows; for not only dost thou mark erudition when it is set before thee, but thou also wisely distrustest thine own knowledge, and questionest of those who are more learned than thou. Touching thy demand of what breed are the Wehr-Wolves, be this mine answer. Thou knowest, that if ye ask of a shepherd how he can distinguish one sheep from another, he tells you that even in their faces he seeth a *distinctio secretio*,[26] the which to a common observer is not visible; and thus, when the vulgar see a wolf, they can but say it is a wolf, and there endeth their cunning. But, by the Lion of St. Mark![27] if ye ask one skilled in the knowledge of four-footed animals, he shall presently discourse to you of the genus and species thereof; make known it's haunts and history, display it's occult properties, and give you a lection upon all that your ancient and modern authors have said concerning it."

"By the Mass now!" interrupted La Jaquette, "and I would fain know the habit in which your Loup Garoux vests him when he is not in his wolfish shape; whether he have slashed cuishes,[28] and—."

"Peace, I pray you peace, good Tailleur," said Doctor Antoine; "it is but rarely that I speak, and even then my discourse is brief, and therefore I beseech you not to mar the words of wisdom which are seldom heard, with thy folly which men may listen to hourly. Touching your Wolves, honest friends, as I was saying, there are five kinds, as Oppianus noteth in his Admonition to Shepherds;[29] of the which, two sorts that rove in the countries of Swecia and the Visigoths, are called *Acmonœ*, but of

---

[26] Distinct secret

[27] A winged lion is the religious symbol for Saint Mark, the apostle of Jesus Christ

[28] Medieval word for armor that protects the thigh

[29] Name of Ancient Greek poet and hexameter poem on hunting

these I will not now speak, but turn me unto those of whose species is the Wehr-Wolf. The first is named Τοξεντερ, or the Shooter, for that he runneth fast, is very bold, howleth fearfully—"

"There is the cry again!" exclaimed Malbois, and as the sounds drew nearer, the Doctor's audience evinced symptoms of alarm, which were rapidly increasing, when a still louder shriek was heard close to the house.

"What, ho! within there!" cried a voice, evidently of one in an agony of terror, "an' ye be men, open the door!" and the next moment it was burst from it's fastenings by the force of a human body falling against it, which dropped without motion upon the floor!

The confusion which this accident created may well be imagined; the Doctor, greatly alarmed, retreated into the fire-place, whence he cried out to the equally scared rustics, "It's a Wehr-Wolf in a human shape, don't touch him, I tell you, but strike him with a fire-fork between the eyes, and he'll turn to a Wolf, and run away! You, Cuirbouilli, out with thy knife, and flay me a piece of his neck, and you'll see the thick wolf-hide under it. For the love of the Saints, neighbours, take care of yourselves, and—"

"Peace, Master Doctor," said Bonvarlet, the only one of the party that had ventured near the stranger, "he breathes yet, for he's a Christian man, like as we are."

"Don't you be too sure of that," replied Du Pilon; "ask him to say his Creed,[30] and his Pater-Noster[31] in Latin."

"Nay, good my master," returned the humane host, pouring some wine down the stranger's throat, and bearing his reviving body to the hearth, "he can scarce speak his mother-tongue, and therefore he's

---

[30] Statement of Christian religious beliefs

[31] The Biblical Lord's Prayer that is recited in the Gospels of Mathew and Luke

no stomach for Latin, so come, thou prince of all Chirurgeons, and bleed me him;[32] and when he comes too, why e'en school him yourself."

Doctor Antoine Du Pilon advanced from his retreat, with considerable reluctance, to attend upon his patient, who was richly habited in the luxuriant fashion of the Court of Francis, and appeared to be a middle-aged man, of handsome features, and commanding presence. As the Doctor, somewhat reassured, began to remove the short cloak to find out the stranger's arm, he started back with affright, and actually roared with pain at receiving a deep scratch from the huge paw of a Wolf, which apparently grew out from his shoulder! "Avaunt thee, Sathanas!"[33] ejaculated Du Pilon, "I told ye how it would be, my masters, that this cursed Wehr-Wolf would bleed us first. By the Porker of St. Anthony! Blessed beast! and he hath clawed me from the *Biceps Flexor Cubiti,* down to the *Os Lunare,* even as a Peasant would plough up a furrow!"

"Ha, ha, ha!" laughed Bonvarlet, holding up the dreaded Wolf's paw, which was yet bleeding, as if it had been recently separated from the animal,— "Here's no Wehr-Wolf, but a brave Hunter, who hath cut off this goodly fore-hand in the forest, with his couteau-de-chasse;[34] but soft," he added, throwing it aside, "he recovers!"

"Pierre!—Henri!" said the stranger, recovering, "where are ye? How far is the King behind us?—Ha! what place is this? and who are ye?" he continued, looking round.

"This, your good worship, is the Chevalier Bayard's Arms, in the Town of St. Yrieux, where your Honour fell, through loss of blood, as I guess by this wound. We were fain to keep the door barred, for fear of the Wehr-Wolves; and we half deemed your Lordship to

---

[32] Reference to bloodletting

[33] Satan

[34] Curved hand knife

be one, at first sight of the great paw you carried, but now, I judge you brought it from the forest."

"Aye! yes, thou art in the right on't," said the stranger, recollecting himself, "'twas in the forest! I tell thee, Host, that I have this night looked upon the Arch-Demon himself!"

"Apage, Lucifer!" ejaculated Du Pilon, devoutly crossing his breast, "and have I received a claw from his fore-foot! I feel the enchantment of Lycanthropy coming over me; I shall be a Wehr-Wolf myself shortly, for what saith Hornhoofius,[35] in his Treatise De Diabolis, lib. xiv. cap. 23,—they who are torn by a Wehr-Wolf—Oh me! Oh me! *Libera nos Domine!*[36] Look to yourselves, neighbours, or I shall raven upon ye all."

"I pray you, Master Doctor," said Bonvarlet, "to let his Lordship tell us his story first, and then we'll hear your's. How was it, fair sir? but take another cup of wine first."

"My tale is brief," answered the stranger; "The King is passing to-night through the Limousin, and, with two of my attendants, I rode forward to prepare for his coming; when, in the darkness of the wood, we were separated, and as I galloped on alone, an enormous Wolf, with fiery flashing eyes, leaped out of a brake before me, with the most fearful howlings, and rushed on me with the speed of lightning."

"Aye," interrupted Du Pilon, "as I told ye, they are called, in the Greekish phrase, Νυχτερι νοι *Κανες,* Dogs of the Night, because of their howlings, and *Τοξευτες,* for that they shoot along."

"Now I pray your honour to proceed, and heed not the Doctor," said Bonvarlet.

"As the Wolf leaped upon my horse," continued the stranger, "I drew my couteau-de-chasse, and severed that huge paw which you found upon me; but as the

---

[35] German author Johannes Hornhoofius who wrote about the spirits of the Harz Mountains

[36] Deliver us Lord!

violence of the blow made the weapon fall, I caught up a large forked branch of a tree, and struck the animal upon the forehead; upon which my horse began to rear and plunge, for where the Wolf stood, I saw, by a momentary glimpse of moonlight, the form of an ancient enemy, who had long since been banished from France, and whom I believe to have died of Famine in the Harz Forest!"

"Lo you there now!" cried Du Pilon, "a blow between the eyes with a forked stick;—said I not so from Philo-Daimones, lib. xcii? Oh! I'm condemned to be a Wehr-Wolf of a verity, and I shall eat those of my most intimate acquaintance the first.—Masters look to yourselves;—*Oh dies infelix!*[37] Oh unhappy man that I am!" and with these words he rushed out of the cottage.

"I think the very Fiend's in Monsieur the Doctor to-night," cried the Host, "for here he's gone off without dressing his honour's wound."

"Heed not that, friend, but do thou provide torches, and assistance, to meet the King; my hurt is but small; but when my horse saw the apparition I told you of, he bounded forward like a wild Russian colt, dragging me through all the briars of the forest, for there seemed a troop of a thousand wolves howling behind us; and at the verge of it he dropped lifeless, and left me, still pursued, to gain the town, weak and wounded as I was!"

"St. Denis[38] be praised now!" said Bonvarlet, "you shewed a good heart, my Lord; but we'll at once set out to meet the King, so neighbours, take each of ye a good pine fagot off the hearth, and call up more help as you go; and Nicolette and Madelene will prepare for our return."

"But," asked the stranger, "where's the Wolf's paw that I brought from the forest?"

---

[37] Oh day of the wretched
[38] Bishop of Paris, beheaded around 250 A.D.

"I cast it aside, my Lord," answered Bonvarlet, "till you had recovered, but I would fain beg it of you as a gift, for I will hang it over my fire-place, and have it's story made into a song by Rowland the Minstrel, and—Mother of God! what is this?" continued he, putting into his guest's hand a human arm, cut off at the elbow, vested in the worn-out sleeve of a hunter's coat, and bleeding freshly at the part where it was dissevered!

"Holy St. Mary!" exclaimed the stranger, regarding the hand attentively, "this is the arm of Gaspar de Marcanville, yet bearing the executioner's brand burnt in the flesh! and he is a Wehr-Wolf!"

"Why," said Bonvarlet, "that's the habit worn by the melancholy Hunter, whose daughter lives at the ruined Chateau yonder. He rarely comes to St. Yrieux, but when he does, he brings more game than any ten of your gentlemen-huntsmen ever did. Come, we'll go seek the daughter of this Man-Wolf, and then on to the forest, for this fellow deserves a stake, and a bundle of fagots, as well as ever Jeanne d'Arc[39] did, in my simple thinking."

They then proceeded to Adéle, at the dilapidated Chateau, and her distress at the foregoing story may better be conceived than described; yet she offered not the slightest assistance to accompanying them to the forest; though when one of the party mentioned their expected meeting with the King, her eyes became suddenly lighted up, and, retiring for a moment, she expressed herself in readiness to attend them.

At the skirts of the forest they found an elderly man, of a strange quaint appearance, couching in the fern like a hare; who called out to them in a squeaking voice, that was at once familiar to all, "Take care of yourselves, good people, for I am a

---

[39] French for Joan of Arc (1412-1431) who was burned alive at the age of 19.

Wehr-Wolf, and shall speedily spring upon some of ye."

"Why that's our Doctor, as I am a sinful man," cried Bonvarlet, "let's try his own cure upon him. Neighbour Malbois, give me a tough forked branch, and I'll disenchant him, I warrant; and you, Cuirbouilli, out with your knife, as though you would skin him:"—and then he continued aloud,—"Oh! honest friend, you're a Wehr-Wolf, are you? why then I'll dispossess the Devil that's in you.—You shall be flayed, and then burned for a wizard."

With that the rustics of St. Yrieux, who enjoyed the jest, fell upon the unhappy Doctor, and, by a sound beating, and other rough usage, so convinced him that he was, not a Wehr-Wolf, that he cried out,— "Praised be St. Gregory,[40] I am a whole man again! Lo I am healed! but my bones feel wondrous sore. Who is he that hath cured me?—by the Mass I am grievously bruised!—thanks to the seraphical[41] Father Francis, the Devil hath gone out of me!"

Whilst the peasants were engaged in searching for the King's party, and the mutilated Wolf, the stranger, who was left with Adele de Marcanville, fainted through loss of blood; and, as she bent over him, and staunched his wounds with her scarf, he said, with a faint voice,—"Fair one! who is it thinkest thou whom thou art so blessedly attending?"

"I wot not," answered she, "but that thou art a man."

"Hear me then, and throw aside these bandages for my dagger, for I am thy father's ancient enemy, the Count de Saintefleur!"

"Heaven forgive you, then!" returned Adele, "for the time of vengeance belongs to it only."

"And it is come," cried a load hoarse voice, as a large Wolf, wounded by the loss of a fore-paw, leaped upon the Count, and put an end to his existence. At

---

[40] Pope Saint Gregory I (540-604)
[41] Type of angel with six wings

the same moment, the royal train, which the peasants had discovered, rode up with flambeaux, and a Knight with a large partizan made a blow at the Wolf, whom Adele vainly endeavoured to preserve, since the stroke was of sufficient power to destroy both. The Wolf gave one terrific howl, and fell backwards in the form of a tall gaunt man, in a hunter's dress; whilst Adele, drawing a packet from her bosom, and offering it to the King, sank lifeless upon the body of her father, Gaspar de Marcanville, the Wehr-Wolf of Limousin.

CAPTAIN FREDERICK MARRYAT
(1792-1848)

Φ

The White Wolf of the Hartz Mountains

Captain Frederick Marryat, author of the venerable horror short stories: "The Story Of The Greek Slave" and "The Legend of the Bell Rock," has given us one of the finest genre tales to come out of the half century in question. In the technical sense we cannot, however, call this a "werewolf" story.

This is due to the male origins of the name. In the French the wolf-man is called the *loup-garou,* in German the *wehr-wolf,* in Old English the wär-wolf and in Portuguese the *lupus-homo. Blackwood's Edinburgh Magazine* (originally called the *Edinburgh Monthly Magazine* when it began in 1817) was the leading publisher of horror tales for the half century in question. The December issue of 1841 gives a fine summary regarding the male origins of the werewolf moniker.

The Anglo-Saxon word *wer,* sometimes written *were,* signifies a man, and they used it in the same way. Sometimes they put it *before* the word to which they joined it, and then they preserved the to, as were-wulf, a *man-wolf—wer*-had, man-hood—*wer*-gyld, man-money, that is, the fine for slaying a man— *wer*-lie, manlike, or manly. Sometimes they put it *after* the word as we do, and then they dropped the *w,* as pleg-ere, a play-man, or player—sæd-*ere,* a sow-*man,* or sower—writ-*ere,* a writ-man, or writer—beat-ere, a beat-man, or beater, that is, a man who is able, or thought to be able, to beat other men—a champion.

In novel form, "Sidonia the Sorceress" by Wilhelm Meinhold in 1849 is a multi-volumed work that gives a fine example of a she-wolf. Previously in this collection we have Catherine Crowe's "A Story of a Weir-Wolf" that centers around a woman accused of being a she-wolf.

In this instance, fifty-eight years before Bram Stoker gave us "Dracula," Captain Frederick Marryat penned this story of a monster rising out of Transylvania. In this case it is a she-wolf.

The story is extracted from Chapter XXXIX of "The Phantom Ship" that first appeared serially in the *New Monthly Magazine*. We begin midway on the second page of this chapter with a query from Philip to Krantz as they sail on the phantom ship.

The White Wolf
of the Hartz Mountains

One morning, as they were sailing between the isles, with less wind than usual, Philip observed:—

"Krantz, you said that there were events in your own life, or connected with it, which would corroborate the mysterious tale I confided to you. Will you now tell me to what you referred?"

"Certainly," replied Krantz; "I have often thought of doing so, but one circumstance or another has hitherto prevented me; this is, however, a fitting opportunity. Prepare therefore to listen to a strange story, quite as strange, perhaps, as your own.

"I take it for granted, that you have heard people speak of the Hartz Mountains," observed Krantz.

"I have never heard people speak of them that I can recollect," replied Philip; "but I have read of them in some book, and of the strange things which have occurred there."

"It is indeed a wild region," rejoined Krantz, "and many strange tales are told of it; but, strange as they are, I have good reason for believing them to be true. I have told you, Philip, that I fully believe in your communion with the other world—that I credit the history of your father, and the lawfulness of your mission; for that we are surrounded, impelled, and worked upon by beings different in their nature from ourselves, I have had full evidence, as you will acknowledge, when I state what has occurred in my own family. Why such malevolent beings as I am about to speak of should be permitted to interfere with us, and punish, I may say, comparatively unoffending mortals, is beyond my comprehension; but that they are so permitted is most certain."

"The great principle of all evil fulfils his work of evil; why, then, not the other minor spirits of the same class?" inquired Philip. "What matters it to us, whether we are tried by, and have to suffer from, the enmity of our fellow-mortals, or whether we are persecuted by beings more powerful and more malevolent than ourselves? We know that we have to work out our salvation, and that we shall be judged according to our strength; if then there be evil spirits who delight to oppress man, there surely must be, as Amine asserts, good spirits, whose delight is to do him service. Whether, then, we have to struggle against our passions only, or whether we have to struggle not only against our passions, but also the dire influence of unseen enemies, we ever struggle with the same odds in our favour, as the good are stronger than the evil which we combat. In either case we are on the vantage ground, whether, as in the first, we fight the good cause singlehanded, or as in the second, although opposed, we have the host of Heaven ranged on our side. Thus are the scales of Divine Justice evenly balanced, and man is still a free agent, as his own virtuous or vicious propensities must ever decide whether he shall gain or lose the victory."

"Most true," replied Krantz, "and now to my history. My father was not born, or originally a resident, in the Hartz Mountains;[1] he was the serf of an Hungarian nobleman, of great possessions, in Transylvania; but, although a serf,[2] he was not by

---

[1] Harz or Hartz mountain range of Germany that is reputed to contain spirits and demons

[2] Indebted servant who cared for the grounds and lands of his lord

any means a poor or illiterate man. In fact, he was rich, and his intelligence and respectability were such, that he had been raised by his lord to the stewardship; but, whoever may happen to be born a serf, a serf must he remain, even though he become a wealthy man; such was the condition of my father.

"My father had been married for about five years; and, by his marriage, had three children—my eldest brother Cæsar, myself (Hermann), and a sister named Marcella. You know, Philip, that Latin is still the language spoken in that country; and that will account for our high sounding names. My mother was a very beautiful woman, unfortunately more beautiful than virtuous: she was seen and admired by the lord of the soil; my father was sent away upon some mission; and, during his absence, my mother, flattered by the attentions, and won by the assiduities, of this nobleman, yielded to his wishes. It so happened that my father returned very unexpectedly, and discovered the intrigue. The evidence of my mother's shame was positive: he surprised her in the company of her seducer!

"Carried away by the impetuosity of his feelings, he watched the opportunity of a meeting taking place between them, and murdered both his wife and her seducer. Conscious that, as a serf, not even the provocation which he had received would be allowed as a justification of his conduct, he hastily collected together what money he could lay his hands upon, and, as we were then in the depth of winter, he put his horses to the sleigh, and taking his children with him, he set off in the middle of the night, and was far away before the tragical circumstance had transpired. Aware that he would be pursued, and that he had no chance of escape if he remained in any portion of his native country (in which the authorities could lay hold of him), he continued his flight without intermission until he had buried himself in the intricacies and seclusion of the Hartz

Mountains. Of course, all that I have now told you I learned afterwards.

"My oldest recollections are knit to a rude, yet comfortable cottage, in which I lived with my father, brother, and sister. It was on the confines of one of those vast forests which cover the northern part of Germany; around it were a few acres of ground, which, during the summer months, my father cultivated, and which, though they yielded a doubtful harvest, were sufficient for our support. In the winter we remained much in doors, for, as my father followed the chase, we were left alone, and the wolves, during that season, incessantly prowled about. My father had purchased the cottage, and land about it, of one of the rude foresters, who gain their livelihood partly by hunting, and partly by burning charcoal, for the purpose of smelting the ore from the neighbouring mines; it was distant about two miles from any other habitation. I can call to mind the whole landscape now: the tall pines which rose up on the mountain above us, and the wide expanse of forest beneath, on the topmost boughs and heads of whose trees we looked down from our cottage, as the mountain below us rapidly descended into the distant valley. In summertime the prospect was beautiful; but during the severe winter, a more desolate scene could not well be imagined.

"I said that, in the winter, my father occupied himself with the chase; every day he left us, and often would he lock the door, that we might not leave the cottage. He had no one to assist him, or to take care of us—indeed, it was not easy to find a female servant who would live in such a solitude; but, could he have found one, my father would not have received her, for he had imbibed a horror of the sex, as the difference of his conduct towards us, his two boys, and my poor little sister, Marcella, evidently proved.

"You may suppose we were sadly neglected; indeed, we suffered much, for my father, fearful that we might come to some harm, would not allow us fuel, when he left the cottage; and we were obliged, therefore, to creep under the heaps of bears'-skins, and there to keep ourselves as warm as we could until he returned in the evening, when a blazing fire was our delight. That my father chose this restless sort of life may appear strange, but the fact was that he could not remain quiet; whether from remorse for having committed murder, or from the misery consequent on his change of situation, or from both combined, he was never happy unless he was in a state of activity. Children, however, when left much to themselves, acquire a thoughtfulness not common to their age. So it was with us; and during the short cold days of winter we would sit silent, longing for the happy hours when the snow would melt, and the leaves burst out, and the birds begin their songs, and when we should again be set at liberty.

"Such was our peculiar and savage sort of life until my brother Caesar was nine, myself seven, and my sister five, years old, when the circumstances occurred on which is based the extraordinary narrative which I am about to relate.

"One evening my father returned home rather later than usual; he had been unsuccessful, and, as the weather was very severe, and many feet of snow were upon the ground, he was not only very cold, but in a very bad humour. He had brought in wood, and we were all three of us gladly assisting each other in blowing on the embers to create the blaze, when he caught poor little Marcella by the arm and threw her aside; the child fell, struck her mouth, and bled very much. My brother ran to raise her up. Accustomed to ill usage, and afraid of my father, she did not dare to cry, but looked up in his face very piteously. My father drew his stool nearer to the hearth, muttered something in abuse of women, and busied himself with the fire, which both my brother and I had deserted when our sister was so unkindly treated.

"A cheerful blaze was soon the result of his exertions; but we did not, as usual, crowd round it. Marcella, still bleeding, retired to a corner, and my brother and I took our seats beside her, while my father hung over the fire gloomily and alone. Such had been our position for about half-an-hour, when the howl of a wolf, close under the window of the cottage, fell on our ears.

"My father started up, and seized his gun: the howl was repeated, he examined the priming,[3] and then hastily left the cottage, shutting the door after him. We all waited (anxiously listening), for we thought that if he succeeded in shooting the wolf, he would return in a better humour; and although he was harsh to all of us, and particularly so to our little sister, still we loved our father, and loved to see him cheerful and happy, for what else had we to look up to? And I may here observe, that perhaps there never were three children who were fonder of each other; we did not, like other children, fight and dispute together; and if, by chance, any disagreement did arise between my elder brother and me, little Marcella would run to us, and kissing us both, seal, through her entreaties, the peace between us. Marcella was a lovely, amiable child; I can recall her beautiful features even now—Alas! poor little Marcella."

"She is dead then?" observed Philip.

"Dead! yes, dead!—but how did she die?—But I must not anticipate, Philip; let me tell my story.

"We waited for some time, but the report of the gun did not reach us, and my elder brother then said, 'Our father has followed the wolf, and will not be back for some time. Marcella, let us wash the blood from your mouth, and then we will leave this corner, and go to the fire and warm ourselves.'

"We did so, and remained there until near midnight, every minute wondering, as it grew later,

---

[3] Gun fuse or igniter

why our father did not return. We had no idea that he was in any danger, but we thought that he must have chased the wolf for a very long time. 'I will look out and see if father is coming,' said my brother Caesar, going to the door.

"'Take care,' said Marcella, 'the wolves must be about now, and we cannot kill them, brother.'

"My brother opened the door very cautiously, and but a few inches; he peeped out.—'I see nothing,' said he, after a time, and once more he joined us at the fire.

"'We have had no supper,' said I, for my father usually cooked the meat as soon as he came home; and during his absence we had nothing but the fragments of the preceding day.

"'And if our father comes home after his hunt, Cæsar,' said Marcella, 'he will be pleased to have some supper; let us cook it for him and for ourselves.'

"Cæsar climbed upon the stool, and reached down some meat—I forget now whether it was venison[4] or bear's meat; but we cut off the usual quantity, and proceeded to dress it, as we used to do under our father's superintendence. We were all busied putting it into the platters before the fire, to await his coming, when we heard the sound of a horn. We listened—there was a noise outside, and a minute afterwards my father entered, ushering in a young female, and a large dark man in a hunter's dress.

"Perhaps I had better now relate, what was only known to me many years afterwards. When my father had left the cottage, he perceived a large white wolf about thirty yards from him; as soon as the animal saw my father, it retreated slowly, growling and snarling. My father followed; the animal did not run, but always kept at some distance; and my father did not like to fire until he was pretty certain

---

[4] Deer meat

that his ball[5] would take effect: thus they went on for
some time, the wolf now leaving my father far
behind, and then stopping and snarling defiance at
him, and then again, on his approach, setting off at
speed.

"Anxious to shoot the animal (for the white wolf is
very rare), my father continued the pursuit for
several hours, during which he continually ascended
the mountain.

"You must know, Philip, that there are peculiar
spots on those mountains which are supposed, and,
as my story will prove, truly supposed, to be
inhabited by the evil influences; they are well known
to the huntsmen, who invariably avoid them. Now,
one of these spots, an open space in the pine forests
above us, had been pointed out to my father as
dangerous on that account. But, whether he
disbelieved these wild stories, or whether, in his
eager pursuit of the chase, he disregarded them, I
know not; certain, however, it is, that he was
decoyed by the white wolf to this open space, when
the animal appeared to slacken her speed. My father
approached, came close up to her, raised his gun to
his shoulder, and was about to fire; when the wolf
suddenly disappeared. He thought that the snow on
the ground must have dazzled his sight, and he let
down his gun to look for the beast—but she was
gone; how she could have escaped over the
clearance, without his seeing her, was beyond his
comprehension.

"Mortified at the ill success of his chase, he was
about to retrace his steps, when he heard the distant
sound of a horn. Astonishment at such a sound—at
such an hour—in such a wilderness, made him
forget for the moment his disappointment, and he
remained riveted to the spot. In a minute the horn
was blown a second time, and at no great distance;
my father stood still, and listened: a third time it was

---

[5] Ball shot of a gun

blown. I forget the term used to express it, but it was the signal which, my father well knew, implied that the party was lost in the woods. In a few minutes more my father beheld a man on horseback, with a female seated on the crupper,[6] enter the cleared space, and ride up to him.

"At first, my father called to mind the strange stories which he had heard of the supernatural beings who were said to frequent these mountains; but the nearer approach of the parties satisfied him that they were mortals like himself.

"As soon as they came up to him, the man who guided the horse accosted him. 'Friend Hunter, you are out late, the better fortune for us: we have ridden far, and are in fear of our lives, which are eagerly sought after. These mountains have enabled us to elude our pursuers; but if we find not shelter and refreshment, that will avail us little, as we must perish from hunger and the inclemency of the night. My daughter, who rides behind me, is now more dead than alive,—say, can you assist us in our difficulty?'

"'My cottage is some few miles distant,' replied my father, 'but I have little to offer you besides a shelter from the weather; to the little I have you are welcome. May I ask whence you come?'

"'Yes, friend, it is no secret now; we have escaped from Transylvania, where my daughter's honour and my life were equally in jeopardy!'

"This information was quite enough to raise an interest in my father's heart. He remembered his own escape: he remembered the loss of his wife's honour, and the tragedy by which it was wound up. He immediately, and warmly, offered all the assistance which he could afford them.

"'There is no time to be lost, then, good sir,' observed the horseman; 'my daughter is chilled with

---

[6] Strap that rests under the tail of a horse to keep a saddle from shifting forward on downhill inclines

the frost, and cannot hold out much longer against the severity of the weather.'

"'Follow me,' replied my father, leading the way towards his home.

"'I was lured away in pursuit of a large white wolf,' observed my father; 'it came to the very window of my hut, or I should not have been out at this time of night.'

"'The creature passed by us just as we came out of the wood,' said the female in a silvery tone.

"'I was nearly discharging my piece at it,' observed the hunter; 'but since it did us such good service, I am glad that I allowed it to escape.'

"In about an hour and a half, during which my father walked at a rapid pace, the party arrived at the cottage, and, as I said before, came in.

"'We are in good time, apparently,' observed the dark hunter, catching the smell of the roasted meat, as he walked to the fire and surveyed my brother and sister, and myself. 'You have young cooks here, Meinheer.'

"'I am glad that we shall not have to wait,' replied my father. 'Come, mistress, seat yourself by the fire; you require warmth after your cold ride.'

"'And where can I put up my horse, Meinheer?' observed the huntsman.

"'I will take care of him,' replied my father, going out of the cottage door.

"The female must, however, be particularly described. She was young, and apparently twenty years of age. She was dressed in a travelling dress, deeply bordered with white fur, and wore a cap of white ermine[7] on her head. Her features were very beautiful, at least I thought so, and so my father has since declared. Her hair was flaxen, glossy and shining, and bright as a mirror; and her mouth, although somewhat large when it was open, showed the most brilliant teeth I have ever beheld. But there

---

[7] Mammal with white fur that is used for coats and hats

was something about her eyes, bright as they were, which made us children afraid; they were so restless, so furtive; I could not at that time tell why, but I felt as if there was cruelty in her eye; and when she beckoned us to come to her, we approached her with fear and trembling. Still she was beautiful, very beautiful. She spoke kindly to my brother and myself, patted our heads, and caressed us; but Marcella would not come near her; on the contrary, she slunk away, and hid herself in the bed, and would not wait for the supper, which half an hour before she had been so anxious for.

"My father, having put the horse into a close shed, soon returned, and supper was placed upon the table. When it was over, my father requested that the young lady would take possession of his bed, and he would remain at the fire, and sit up with her father. After some hesitation on her part, this arrangement was agreed to, and I and my brother crept into the other bed with Marcella, for we had as yet always slept together.

"But we could not sleep; there was something so unusual, not only in seeing strange people, but in having those people sleep at the cottage, that we were bewildered. As for poor little Marcella, she was quiet, but I perceived that she trembled during the whole night, and sometimes I thought that she was checking a sob. My father had brought out some spirits, which he rarely used, and he and the strange hunter remained drinking and talking before the fire. Our ears were ready to catch the slightest whisper—so much was our curiosity excited.

"'You said you came from Transylvania?' observed my father.

"'Even so, Meinheer,' replied the hunter. 'I was a serf to the noble house of —; my master would insist upon my surrendering up my fair girl to his wishes; it ended in my giving him a few inches of my hunting-knife.'

"'We are countrymen, and brothers in misfortune,' replied my father, taking the huntsman's hand, and pressing it warmly.

"'Indeed! Are you, then, from that country?'

"'Yes; and I too have fled for my life. But mine is a melancholy tale.'

"'Your name?' inquired the hunter.

"'Krantz.'

"'What! Krantz of — I have heard your tale; you need not renew your grief by repeating it now. Welcome, most welcome, Meinheer, and, I may say, my worthy kinsman. I am your second cousin, Wilfred of Barnsdorf,' cried the hunter, rising up and embracing my father.

"They filled their horn mugs to the brim, and drank to one another, after the German fashion. The conversation was then carried on in a low tone; all that we could collect from it was, that our new relative and his daughter were to take up their abode in our cottage, at least for the present. In about an hour they both fell back in their chairs, and appeared to sleep.

"'Marcella, dear, did you hear?' said my brother in a low tone.

"'Yes,' replied Marcella, in a whisper; 'I heard all. Oh! brother, I cannot bear to look upon that woman—I feel so frightened.'

"My brother made no reply, and shortly afterwards we were all three fast asleep.

"When we awoke the next morning, we found that the hunter's daughter had risen before us. I thought she looked more beautiful than ever. She came up to little Marcella and caressed her; the child burst into tears, and sobbed as if her heart would break.

"But, not to detain you with too long a story, the huntsman and his daughter were accommodated in the cottage. My father and he went out hunting daily, leaving Christina with us. She performed all the household duties; was very kind to us children; and, gradually, the dislike even of little Marcella wore away. But a great change took place in my father; he appeared to have conquered his aversion to the sex, and was most attentive to Christina. Often, after her father and we were in bed, would he sit up with her, conversing in a low tone by the fire. I ought to have mentioned, that my father and the huntsman Wilfred, slept in another portion of the cottage, and that the bed which he formerly occupied, and which was in the same room as ours, had been given up to the use of Christina. These visitors had been about three weeks at the cottage, when, one night, after we children had been sent to bed, a consultation was held. My father had asked Christina in marriage, and had obtained both her own consent and that of Wilfred; after this a conversation took place, which was, as nearly as I can recollect, as follows:—

"'You may take my child, Meinheer Krantz, and my blessing with her, and I shall then leave you and seek some other habitation—it matters little where.'

"'Why not remain here, Wilfred?'

"'No, no, I am called elsewhere; let that suffice, and ask no more questions. You have my child.'

"'I thank you for her, and will duly value her; but there is one difficulty.'

"'I know what you would say; there is no priest here in this wild country: true; neither is there any law to bind; still must some ceremony pass between you, to satisfy a father. Will you consent to marry her after my fashion? if so, I will marry you directly.'

"'I will,' replied my father.

"'Then take her by the hand. Now, Meinheer, swear.'

"'I swear,' repeated my father.

"'By all the spirits of the Hartz Mountains—'

"'Nay, why not by Heaven?' interrupted my father.

"'Because it is not my humour,' rejoined Wilfred; 'if I prefer that oath, less binding perhaps, than another, surely you will not thwart me.'

"'Well, be it so then; have your humour. Will you make me swear by that in which I do not believe?'

"'Yet many do so, who in outward appearance are Christians,' rejoined Wilfred; 'say, will you be married, or shall I take my daughter away with me?'

"'Proceed,' replied my father, impatiently.

"'I swear by all the spirits of the Hartz Mountains, by all their power for good or for evil, that I take Christina for my wedded wife; that I will ever protect her, cherish her, and love her; that my hand shall never be raised against her to harm her.'

"My father repeated the words after Wilfred.

"'And if I fail in this my vow, may all the vengeance of the spirits fall upon me and upon my children; may they perish by the vulture, by the wolf, or other beasts of the forest; may their flesh be torn from their limbs, and their bones blanch in the wilderness; all this I swear.'

"My father hesitated, as he repeated the last words; little Marcella could not restrain herself, and as my father repeated the last sentence, she burst into tears. This sudden interruption appeared to discompose the party, particularly my father; he spoke harshly to the child, who controlled her sobs, burying her face under the bedclothes.

"Such was the second marriage of my father. The next morning, the hunter Wilfred mounted his horse, and rode away.

"My father resumed his bed, which was in the same room as ours; and things went on much as before the marriage, except that our new mother-in-law did not show any kindness towards us; indeed, during my father's absence, she would often beat us, particularly little Marcella, and her eyes would flash fire, as she looked eagerly upon the fair and lovely child.

"One night, my sister awoke me and my brother.

"'What is the matter?' said Cæsar.

"'She has gone out,' whispered Marcella.

"'Gone out!'

"'Yes, gone out at the door, in her night-clothes,' replied the child; 'I saw her get out of bed, look at my father to see if he slept, and then she went out at the door.'

"What could induce her to leave her bed, and all undressed to go out, in such bitter wintry weather, with the snow deep on the ground, was to us incomprehensible; we lay awake, and in about an hour we heard the growl of a wolf, close under the window.

"'There is a wolf,' said Cæsar; 'she will be torn to pieces.'

"'Oh, no!' cried Marcella.

"In a few minutes afterwards our mother-in-law appeared; she was in her night-dress, as Marcella had stated. She let down the latch of the door, so as to make no noise, went to a pail of water, and washed her face and hands, and then slipped into the bed where my father lay.

"We all three trembled, we hardly knew why, but we resolved to watch the next night: we did so—and not only on the ensuing night, but on many others, and always at about the same hour, would our mother-in-law rise from her bed, and leave the cottage—and after she was gone, we invariably heard the growl of a wolf under our window, and always saw her, on her return, wash herself before she retired to bed. We observed, also, that she seldom sat down to meals, and that when she did, she appeared to eat with dislike; but when the meat was taken down, to be prepared for dinner, she would often furtively put a raw piece into her mouth.

"My brother Cæsar was a courageous boy; he did not like to speak to my father until he knew more. He resolved that he would follow her out, and ascertain what she did. Marcella and I endeavoured to dissuade him from this project; but he would not be controlled, and, the very next night he lay down in his clothes, and as soon as our mother-in-law had left the cottage, he jumped up, took down my father's gun, and followed her.

"You may imagine in what a state of suspense Marcella and I remained, during his absence. After a few minutes, we heard the report of a gun. It did not awaken my father, and we lay trembling with anxiety. In a minute afterwards we saw our mother-in-law enter the cottage—her dress was bloody. I put my hand to Marcella's mouth to prevent her crying out, although I was myself in great alarm. Our mother-in-law approached my father's bed, looked to see if he was asleep, and then went to the chimney, and blew up the embers into a blaze.

"'Who is there?' said my father, waking up.

"'Lie still, dearest,' replied my mother-in-law, 'it is only me; I have lighted the fire to warm some water; I am not quite well.'

"My father turned round and was soon asleep; but we watched our mother-in-law. She changed her linen, and threw the garments she had worn into the fire; and we then perceived that her right leg was bleeding profusely, as if from a gun-shot wound. She bandaged it up, and then dressing herself, remained before the fire until the break of day.

"Poor little Marcella, her heart beat quick as she pressed me to her side—so indeed did mine. Where was our brother, Cæsar? How did my mother-in-law receive the wound unless from his gun? At last my father rose, and then, for the first time I spoke, saying, 'Father, where is my brother, Cæsar?'

"'Your brother!' exclaimed he, 'why, where can he be?'

"'Merciful Heaven! I thought as I lay very restless last night,' observed our mother-in-law, 'that I heard somebody open the latch of the door; and, dear me, husband, what has become of your gun?'

"My father cast his eyes up above the chimney, and perceived that his gun was missing. For a moment he looked perplexed, then seizing a broad axe, he went out of the cottage without saying another word.

"He did not remain away from us long: in a few minutes he returned, bearing in his arms the mangled body of my poor brother; he laid it down, and covered up his face.

"My mother-in-law rose up, and looked at the body, while Marcella and I threw ourselves by its side wailing and sobbing bitterly.

"'Go to bed again, children,' said she sharply. 'Husband,' continued she, 'your boy must have taken the gun down to shoot a wolf, and the animal has been too powerful for him. Poor boy! he has paid dearly for his rashness.'

"My father made no reply; I wished to speak—to tell all—but Marcella, who perceived my intention, held me by the arm, and looked at me so imploringly, that I desisted.

"My father, therefore, was left in his error; but Marcella and I, although we could not comprehend it, were conscious that our mother-in-law was in some way connected with my brother's death.

"That day my father went out and dug a grave, and when he laid the body in the earth, he piled up stones over it, so that the wolves should not be able to dig it up. The shock of this catastrophe was to my poor father very severe; for several days he never went to the chase, although at times he would utter bitter anathemas[8] and vengeance against the wolves.

"But during this time of mourning on his part, my mother-in-law's nocturnal wanderings continued with the same regularity as before.

"At last, my father took down his gun, to repair to the forest; but he soon returned, and appeared much annoyed.

"'Would you believe it, Christina, that the wolves—perdition to the whole race—have actually contrived to dig up the body of my poor boy, and now there is nothing left of him but his bones?'

---

[8] Curses

"'Indeed!' replied my mother-in-law. Marcella looked at me, and I saw in her intelligent eye all she would have uttered.

"'A wolf growls under our window every night, father,' said I.

"'Aye, indeed?—why did you not tell me, boy?—wake me the next time you hear it.'

"I saw my mother-in-law turn away; her eyes flashed fire, and she gnashed her teeth.

"My father went out again, and covered up with a larger pile of stones the little remnants of my poor brother which the wolves had spared. Such was the first act of the tragedy.

"The spring now came on: the snow disappeared, and we were permitted to leave the cottage; but never would I quit, for one moment, my dear little sister, to whom, since the death of my brother, I was more ardently attached than ever; indeed I was afraid to leave her alone with my mother-in-law, who appeared to have a particular pleasure in ill-treating the child. My father was now employed upon his little farm, and I was able to render him some assistance.

"Marcella used to sit by us while we were at work, leaving my mother-in-law alone in the cottage. I ought to observe that, as the spring advanced, so did my mother-in-law decrease her nocturnal rambles, and that we never heard the growl of the wolf under the window after I had spoken of it to my father.

"One day, when my father and I were in the field, Marcella being with us, my mother-in-law came out, saying that she was going into the forest, to collect some herbs my father wanted, and that Marcella must go to the cottage and watch the dinner. Marcella went, and my mother-in-law soon disappeared in the forest, taking a direction quite contrary to that in which the cottage stood, and leaving my father and I, as it were, between her and Marcella.

"About an hour afterwards we were startled by shrieks from the cottage, evidently the shrieks of little Marcella. 'Marcella has burnt herself, father,' said I, throwing down my spade. My father threw down his, and we both hastened to the cottage. Before we could gain the door, out darted a large white wolf, which fled with the utmost celerity. My father had no weapon; he rushed into the cottage, and there saw poor little Marcella expiring: her body was dreadfully mangled, and the blood pouring from it had formed a large pool on the cottage floor. My father's first intention had been to seize his gun and pursue, but he was checked by this horrid spectacle; he knelt down by his dying child, and burst into tears: Marcella could just look kindly on us for a few seconds, and then her eyes were closed in death.

"My father and I were still hanging over my poor sister's body, when my mother-in-law came in. At the dreadful sight she expressed much concern, but she did not appear to recoil from the sight of blood, as most women do.

"'Poor child!' said she, 'it must have been that great white wolf which passed me just now, and frightened me so—she's quite dead, Krantz.'

"'I know it—I know it!' cried my father in agony.

"I thought my father would never recover from the effects of this second tragedy: he mourned bitterly over the body of his sweet child, and for several days would not consign it to its grave, although frequently requested by my mother-in-law to do so. At last he yielded, and dug a grave for her close by that of my poor brother, and took every precaution that the wolves should not violate her remains.

"I was now really miserable, as I lay alone in the bed which I had formerly shared with my brother and sister. I could not help thinking that my mother-in-law was implicated in both their deaths, although I could not account for the manner; but I no longer felt afraid of her: my little heart was full of hatred and revenge.

"The night after my sister had been buried, as I lay awake, I perceived my mother-in-law get up and go out of the cottage. I waited some time, then dressed myself, and looked out through the door, which I half opened. The moon shone bright, and I could see the spot where my brother and my sister had been buried; and what was my horror, when I perceived my mother-in-law busily removing the stones from Marcella's grave.

"She was in her white night-dress, and the moon shone full upon her. She was digging with her hands, and throwing away the stones behind her with all the ferocity of a wild beast. It was some time before I could collect my senses and decide what I should do. At last, I perceived that she had arrived at the body, and raised it up to the side of the grave. I could bear it no longer; I ran to my father and awoke him.

"'Father! father!' cried I, 'dress yourself, and get your gun.'

"'What!' cried my father, 'the wolves are there, are they?'

"He jumped out of bed, threw on his clothes, and in his anxiety did not appear to perceive the absence of his wife. As soon as he was ready, I opened the door, he went out, and I followed him.

"Imagine his horror, when (unprepared as he was for such a sight) he beheld, as he advanced towards the grave, not a wolf, but his wife, in her night-dress, on her hands and knees, crouching by the body of my sister, and tearing off large pieces of the flesh, and devouring them with all the avidity of a wolf. She was too busy to be aware of our approach. My father dropped his gun, his hair stood on end; so did mine; he breathed heavily, and then his breath for a time stopped. I picked up the gun and put it into his hand. Suddenly he appeared as if concentrated rage had restored him to double vigour; he leveled his piece, fired, and with a loud shriek, down fell the wretch whom he had fostered in his bosom.

"'God of Heaven!' cried my father, sinking down upon the earth in a swoon, as soon as he had discharged his gun.

"I remained some time by his side before he recovered. 'Where am I?' said he, 'what has happened?—Oh!—yes, yes! I recollect now. Heaven forgive me!'

"He rose and we walked up to the grave; what again was our astonishment and horror to find that instead of the dead body of my mother-in-law, as we expected, there was lying over the remains of my poor sister, a large, white she wolf.

"'The white wolf!' exclaimed my father, 'the white wolf which decoyed me into the forest—I see it all now—I have dealt with the spirits of the Hartz Mountains.'

"For some time my father remained in silence and deep thought. He then carefully lifted up the body of my sister, replaced it in the grave, and covered it over as before, having struck the head of the dead animal with the heel of his boot, and raving like a madman. He walked back to the cottage, shut the door, and threw himself on the bed; I did the same, for I was in a stupor of amazement.

"Early in the morning we were both roused by a loud knocking at the door, and in rushed the hunter Wilfred.

"'My daughter!—man—my daughter!—where is my daughter!' cried he in a rage.

"'Where the wretch, the fiend, should be, I trust,' replied my father, starting up and displaying equal choler; 'where she should be—in hell!—Leave this cottage or you may fare worse.'

"'Ha—ha!' replied the hunter, 'would you harm a potent spirit of the Hartz Mountains. Poor mortal, who must needs wed a weir wolf.'

"'Out demon! I defy thee and thy power.'

"'Yet shall you feel it; remember your oath—your solemn oath—never to raise your hand against her to harm her.'

"'I made no compact with evil spirits.'

"'You did; and if you failed in your vow, you were to meet the vengeance of the spirits. Your children were to perish by the vulture, the wolf—'

"'Out, out, demon!'

"'And their bones blanch in the wilderness. Ha!— ha!'

"My father, frantic with rage, seized his axe, and raised it over Wilfred's head to strike.

"'All this I swear,' continued the huntsman, mockingly.

"The axe descended; but it passed through the form of the hunter, and my father lost his balance, and fell heavily on the floor.

"'Mortal!' said the hunter, striding over my father's body, 'we have power over those only who have committed murder. You have been guilty of a double murder—you shall pay the penalty attached to your marriage vow. Two of your children are gone; the third is yet to follow—and follow them he will, for your oath is registered. Go—it were kindness to kill thee—your punishment is—that you live!'

"With these words the spirit disappeared. My father rose from the floor, embraced me tenderly, and knelt down in prayer.

"The next morning he quitted the cottage for ever. He took me with him and bent his steps to Holland, where we safely arrived. He had some little money with him; but he had not been many days in Amsterdam before he was seized with a brain fever, and died raving mad. I was put into the Asylum, and afterwards was sent to sea before the mast. You now know all my history. The question is, whether I am to pay the penalty of my father's oath? I am myself perfectly convinced that, in some way or another, I shall."

On the twenty-second day the high land of the south of Sumatra was in view; as there were no vessels in sight, they resolved to keep their course through the Straits, and run for Pulo Penang, which they expected, as their vessel laid so close to the wind, to reach in seven or eight days. By constant exposure, Philip and Krantz were now so bronzed, that with their long beards and Mussulman[9] dresses, they might easily have passed off for natives. They had steered during the whole of the days exposed to a burning sun; they had lain down and slept in the dew of night, but their health had not suffered.

But for several days, since he had confided the history of his family to Philip, Krantz had become silent and melancholy; his usual flow of spirits had vanished, and Philip had often questioned him as to the cause. As they entered the Straits, Philip talked of what they should do upon their arrival at Goa. When Krantz gravely replied, "For some days, Philip, I have had a presentiment that I shall never see that city."

"You are out of health, Krantz," replied Philip.

"No; I am in sound health, body and mind. I have endeavoured to shake off the presentiment, but in vain; there is a warning voice that continually tells me that I shall not be long with you. Philip, will you oblige me by making me content on one point: I have gold about my person which may be useful to you; oblige me by taking it, and securing it on your own."

"What nonsense, Krantz."

"It is no nonsense, Philip. Have you not had your warnings? Why should I not have mine? You know that I have little fear in my composition, and that I care not about death; but I feel the presentiment which I speak of more strongly every hour. It is some kind spirit who would warn me to prepare for another world. Be it so. I have lived long enough in this world to leave it without regret; although to part with you and Amine, the only two now dear to me, is painful, I acknowledge."

"May not this arise from over-exertion and fatigue, Krantz? Consider how much excitement you

---

[9] Religious outfit of a Muslim

have laboured under within these last four months. Is not that enough to create a corresponding depression? Depend upon it, my dear friend, such is the fact."

"I wish it were—but I feel otherwise, and there is a feeling of gladness connected with the idea that I am to leave this world, arising from another presentiment, which equally occupies my mind."

"Which is?"

"I hardly can tell you; but Amine and you are connected with it. In my dreams I have seen you meet again; but it has appeared to me, as if a portion of your trial was purposely shut from my sight in dark clouds; and I have asked, 'May not I see what is there concealed?'—and an invisible has answered, "No! 'twould make you wretched. Before these trials take place, you will be summoned away'—and then I have thanked Heaven, and felt resigned."

"These are the imaginings of a disturbed brain, Krantz; that I am destined to suffering may be true; but why Amine should suffer, or why you, young, in full health and vigour, should not pass your days in peace, and live to a good old age, there is no cause for believing. You will be better to-morrow."

"Perhaps so," replied Krantz;—"but still you must yield to my whim, and take the gold. If I am wrong, and we do arrive safe, you know, Philip, you can let me have it back," observed Krantz, with a faint smile—"but you forget, our water is nearly out, and we must look out for a rill on the coast to obtain a fresh supply."

"I was thinking of that when you commenced this unwelcome topic. We had better look out for the water before dark, and as soon as we have replenished our jars, we will make sail again."

At the time that this conversation took place, they were on the eastern side of the Strait, about forty miles to the northward. The interior of the coast was rocky and mountainous, but it slowly descended to low land of alternate forest and jungles, which continued to the beach: the country appeared to be uninhabited. Keeping close in to the shore, they discovered, after two hours' run, a fresh stream which burst in a cascade from the mountains, and swept its devious course through the jungle, until it poured its tribute into the waters of the Strait.

They ran close in to the mouth of the stream, lowered the sails, and pulled the peroqua[10] against the current, until they had advanced far enough to assure them that the water was quite fresh. The jars were soon filled, and they were again thinking of pushing off; when, enticed by the beauty of the spot, the coolness of the fresh water, and wearied with their long confinement on board of the peroqua, they proposed to bathe—a luxury hardly to be appreciated by those who have not been in a similar situation.

They threw off their Mussulman dresses, and plunged into the stream, where they remained for some time. Krantz was the first to get out; he complained of feeling chilled, and he walked on to the banks where their clothes had been laid. Philip also approached nearer to the beach, intending to follow him.

"And now, Philip," said Krantz, "this will be a good opportunity for me to give you the money. I will open my sash, and pour it out, and you can put it into your own before you put it on."

Philip was standing in the water, which was about level with his waist.

"Well, Krantz," said he, "I suppose if it must be so, it must; but it appears to me an idea so ridiculous—however, you shall have your own way."

Philip quitted the run, and sat down by Krantz, who was already busy in shaking the doubloons[11] out of the folds of his sash; at last he said—

"I believe, Philip, you have got them all, now?—I feel satisfied."

---

[10] Agile and quick ship
[11] Gold coins

"What danger there can be to you, which I am not equally exposed to, I cannot conceive," replied Philip; "however—"

Hardly had he said these words, when there was a tremendous roar—a rush like a mighty wind through the air—a blow which threw him on his back—a loud cry—and a contention. Philip recovered himself, and perceived the naked form of Krantz carried off with the speed of an arrow by an enormous tiger through the jungle. He watched with distended eyeballs; in a few seconds the animal and Krantz had disappeared!

"God of Heaven! would that Thou hadst spared me this," cried Philip, throwing himself down in agony on his face. "Oh! Krantz, my friend—my brother—too sure was your presentiment. Merciful God! have pity—but Thy will be done;" and Philip burst into a flood of tears.

For more than an hour did he remain fixed upon the spot, careless and indifferent to the danger by which he was surrounded. At last, somewhat recovered, he rose, dressed himself, and then again sat down—his eyes fixed upon the clothes of Krantz, and the gold which still lay on the sand.

"He would give me that gold. He foretold his doom. Yes! yes! it was his destiny, and it has been fulfilled. *His bones will bleach in the wilderness*, and the spirit-hunter and his wolfish daughter are avenged."

LIST OF SHORT STORIES CONSIDERED FOR THIS ANTHOLOGY

Anonymous
    1821 Hallowe'en in Germany, or Walpurgis Night
    (passing reference)

Catherine Crowe (1803-1876)
    1846 A Story of a Weir-Wolf

H. Laurence
    1827 Norman of the Strong Arm: A Tale of the
    Sanctuary of Westminster

Sutherland Menzies
    1838 Hugues the Wer-Wolf: A Kentish Legend of
    the Middle Ages

Frederick Marryat
    1839 The White Wolf of the Hartz Mountains
    (Chapter 39) from "The Phantom Ship"

Leitch Ritchie
    1830 The Man-Wolf

Joseph Snowe
    1839 Ursel. The Water-Wolf

Richard Thomson
    1828 The Wehr-Wolf: A Legend of the Limousin

INDEX OF REAL NAMES

Stone, Elizabeth–17
Swift, Jonathan–50

T
Thomson, Richard–113
Tilbury, Gervoise of–44
Thiers, Louise-Adolphe–61
Tobit–126

OTHER BOTTLETREE TITLES

The Best Horror Short Stories 1800-1849
A Classic Horror Anthology
(www.BottletreeBooks.com/BestHorrorShortStories1800.htm)

After reading over 300 horror short stories from such key periodical magazines such as *Blackwood's* and *Atkinson's Casket*, Andrew Barger has assembled an outstanding collection of horror stories that he believes are the very best from 1800-1849. The collection includes the scholarly review of each story by Andrew Barger. The stories are sure to keep you awake at night.

Edgar Allan Poe Annotated and Illustrated
Entire Stories and Poems
(www.BottletreeBooks.com/EdgarAllanPoe.htm)

For the first time in one compilation are background information for Poe's stories and poems, annotations, foreign word translations, illustrations, photographs of individuals Poe wrote about, and poetry to Poe from his many romantic interests. Consider some of the tales and poems included: Annabel Lee, The Bells, The Black Cat, [The Bloodhounds], The Cask of Amontillado, The Conqueror Worm, A Descent into the Maelstrom, The Fall of the House of Usher, The Gold-Bug, The Haunted Palace, Lenore, The Masque of the Red Death, MS. Found in a Bottle, Murders in the Rue Morgue, The Pit and the Pendulum, The Premature Burial, The Purloined Letter, [The Rats of Park Theatre], The Raven, Some Words with a Mummy, he Tell-Tale Heart, and Thou Art the Man. The classic illustrations are by Gustave Dore and Harry Clarke, with a poignant introduction by Andrew Barger.

Leo Tolstoy's 20 Greatest Short Stories
Annotated
(www.BottletreeBooks.com/TolstoyShortStories.htm)

"Anna Karenina" and "War and Peace" revealed Leo Tolstoy to be one of the greatest writers in modern history. Few, however, have read his wonderful short stories. Now, in one collection, are the greatest short stories of Tolstoy, which give a snapshot of Russia and its people in the late 19th century. Annotations are included of difficult Russian terms. There is also a Tolstoy biography at the start of the book with photos of Tolstoy's relatives. Read these short classics today!

Facebook Fanatic
(www.BottletreeBooks.com/Facebook.htm)

Make your face royalty on Facebook. Get insanely popular. Buzz a band or book. Zoom a political career or film. Secure privacy in every area. With over 100 million users Facebook is one of the world's largest social networking sites and it has been making major changes. Are you wondering about all those new Facebook applications? Feel lost and overwhelmed? Concerned about privacy? Don't be! "Facebook Fanatic" is a guide on all areas of Facebook. Dominate it instead of being just part of it.

Bottletree®

BottletreeBooks.com